THE MAN

Memoirs of a Cinema Projectionist

THE MAN IN THE BOX
MEMOIRS OF A CINEMA PROJECTIONIST

Geoffrey H. Carder

UNITED WRITERS
Cornwall

UNITED WRITERS PUBLICATIONS LTD
Trevail Mill, Zennor, St. Ives, Cornwall.

ISBN 901976 80 6

Printed in Great Britain by
United Writers Publications Ltd
Cornwall

To Douglas Gordon Carder

ACKNOWLEDGEMENTS

Sincere appreciation and acknowledgement to:

Douglas Gordon Carder (Cinema technician/projectionist for his co-operation and photographs.)

Cinema Theatre Association (to Marcus Eavis, Secretary and Keith Skone, Archivist.)

The Cinema Organ Society (with special thanks to Tony Moss for his help and indisputable interest in this work.)

Hampshire Chronicle (for prompt co-operation and encouragement from Editor, Monica Woodhouse.)

Cinema TV Today (to Ian A. Freeman, Managing Editor, for 'free-run' of his archives, as arranged by courtesy of David Lewin.)

B.F.I. (British Film Institute) (The National Film Archive for help and guidance.)

Robin Richmond (Cinema organist and BBC broadcaster, for help and guidance.)

Acknowledgement also to *all* manufacturers of cinematic and allied equipment referred to in this work, including Western Electric and R.C.A. sound systems, Ross, Walturdaw, G.B./Kalee, Simplex, B.T.H. and other projectors.

F.T.S. Film Transport service.

Philip C. Baldwin MIMII (Publisher/Editor-in-Chief *Home Organist & Leisure Music* for his interest and guidance.)

John D. Sharp (for his co-operation and photographs.)

CONTENTS

THE MAGIC OF THE SILVER SCREEN.
My introduction to THE ELECTRIC PICTURE THEATRE:
The showman who held me in awe and lectured for hours on
the code of the theatre. The fanatical exhibitor who lived by
the rule, 'come hell or high water, the show must go on!' THE
LAST DAYS OF THE 'SILENT' PICTURE: The eccentric
character on the tinkling piano — The three-piece orchestra
and the old man who failed to hit the high notes on his trumpet.
The hand-turned projectors and other primitive equipment. The
highly inflammable nitrate film and the constant danger of fire.
Why the early projectionist invariably wore a cap in the box.
The jack-of-all-trades man — the bill-posting — the seat repairer
— the boiler man — cashier — attendant — runner — manager,
etc. THE INDEPENDENT CINEMA: The intrigue, pathos, and
revealing love-life of the unconventional staff of the independent
house. The early disc-talkies. THE CIRCUIT CINEMA: The big
organisations rear their massive heads. The man in the box
revalues his status, while the small exhibitor fights to 'stay in the
picture'.

THE GOLDEN ERA OF SOUND ON FILM.
The introduction of the MIGHTY MULTI-COLOURED PIPE
ORGAN: The temperamental organist and his devotion to drink.
HARD-CORE HEAD-OFFICE MANAGEMENT LAY DOWN
THE LAW: The ever-increasing technical burdens on the pro-

jectionist. New rules and regulations. The feud with the management and the prolonged fight for technical status and Union recognition. THE HAUNTED CINEMA: The 'unaccountable happenings' at the Super Cinema. The sound engineer who was afraid to stay in the projection room. The eerie characters who ran screaming from the darkened cinema in the middle of the night.

INTRODUCTION

From the very first days of animated pictures, glamour has surrounded the cinema industry. In these 'straight from the shoulder' memoirs, I have no occasion (in this book, anyway) to refer at any great length to the obvious glamour and exploitation of the stars, nor indeed to the rise of legendary film studios and picture-makers in general. To endeavour to do so I feel, would be an injustice to those for whom I have the greatest admiration and respect, yet have little or no part in these memoirs.

No, this book is, I hope, at least an honest attempt to 'put in the picture' the seemingly forgotten loyal 'army' of film technicians without whom the entire film industry, not least, the great stars themselves, would never have existed. In other words, the Cinema Projectionist — the lone character in the projection room; the final, yet vital link in bringing the end-product to the screen.

In conclusion, it is my sincere belief, whether the reader is but remotely connected with the cinema, the revelations in this book will prove at least enlightening, even nostalgic. At best, astonishing, provocative and even daring, but I trust, never — never boring.

This brings me to a point which I feel should be made perfectly clear. For obvious reasons, names, places, etc., will be of necessity, fictitious, for this is, after all, an authentic narrative of my life in the cinema, and I have no desire to embarrass anyone intentionally or otherwise.

Thank you.

SECTION ONE

THE MAGIC OF THE SILVER SCREEN

It is an unfortunate quirk of our existence, is it not, that very early in life we are *certain* (or think we are!) of what we want. Later, perhaps much later, however, we realise only too well, this is not the case at all. Indeed, we can but only reflect in retrospect when considering this problem in later years. For by the very nature of things, it is but by experience alone, we are bestowed with wisdom; and then, only then, are we forced to admit, perhaps reluctantly, our forefathers experience and forethought is alas also worthy of consideration in determining our future contribution to society.

Be that as it may, and being no exception to any other headstrong school-leaver deciding his future career, I flaunted my parents advice to become a doctor or schoolmaster and chose instead to enter the hazardous world of entertainment. Frankly, I was drawn irresistibly to the 'magic of the movies'. Come what might, I simply had to work in a picture theatre.

Perhaps the fact that my beloved family had endured far too long the purgatory of sitting through repeat performances of my home cinema exhibitions of Charlie Chaplin, Mary Pickford, Buster Keaton, etc., from my primitive, hand-turned, silent film projector, had no little significance in their decision to 'let me have my own way'. Perhaps too, 'the die was cast' when our pet budgerigar was found dead in its cage, apparently poisoned by the fumes from the makeshift carbide acetylene light apparatus I used for the projection of my pictures. Moreover, the occasion when the film ignited in the projector one night and was hastily dispatched through the nearest window, the fire from which was witnessed several miles away, must also have been a good argument to concede to

10

my request to go into the picture theatre.

Thus resolved, the eventful day arrived when my father marched me off to meet a local film exhibitor.

The light of day was giving way to the shadows of night as we reached our destination outside THE ELECTRIC PICTURE THEATRE. For a while I stood spellbound (I suppose open-mouthed) gazing at the blaze of electric lights which left the beholder in no doubt whatsoever as to which picture house this represented. It was only the immediate appearance of a dapper, middle-aged man in evening attire that drew my hypnotic attention from the electric lights, to look this time, apprehensively in his direction. As the penguin-like character approached, his right hand shot out in welcome and he proffered a smile which undoubtedly endeared him to his patrons. His hair, the bulk of which was brushed straight back from his forehead, was jet black save that at his temples where a slight greyness appeared in harmony with the rest of his adornment.

"Good evening, Mr Carder," he greeted my father cordially. Then to me he said as he cocked an eyebrow, "So this is the young man who wants to work in pictures, eh?"

"Yes please," I recall saying rather stupidly as my father went on to explain my almost fanatical fascination for films and the eventual desire to own a picture theatre.

'Hm," uttered the 'big' man himself as with careful deliberation (not unlike George Raft in his early movies) he extracted a silver cigarette case from within his silken jacket and deftly flicking it open, proffered my father a cigarette before placing one between his own lips.

A moment later we were escorted down a flight of stone steps to an inadequately ventilated cellar that served as an office, the walls of which displayed numerous photographs of film stars and trade exploitation notices. The manager placed his immaculate frame behind a ridiculously large desk for such a confined space and indicated a couple of ex-auditorium chairs for our own use. "Well, Mr Carder," he began at length, "while I have no intention of embellishing the opportunities in the picture industry today, on the other hand, I must say there are indeed, some very attractive rewards for anyone as obviously keen as your son, here."

Nonetheless, from that moment on, my future employer left me — and my father for that matter — in do doubt whatsoever as to what was expected of me, if I were to make the grade. Indeed, it was not until some two hours later, that the immaculate one slapped his carefully-manicured hands upon the desk before him and exclaimed, "There is far more to it than that, of course," he had smiled benevolently in my direction, "but all in good time, eh, Mr Carder?"

My father returned that whimsical smile of his he reserved for this kind of situation, I remember. He nodded his head thoughtfully as the other man said earnestly: "Now come, let me show you around."

A pretty usherette with blonde hair, stood respectfully aside as we entered an extravagantly scent-sprayed auditorium. Even from here, in spite of the music which accompanied an early silent picture, I was aware of the clatter of celluloid from the projection room above and behind an upper slope of seats, boastfully called The Circle. I turned my head, fascinated by the fluctuating shaft of light from one of the projection portholes. "Come," whispered a voice as we proceeded further along a narrow aisle towards the screen upon which performed the animated shadows of some of the stars I had seen displayed on the walls in the manager's office. The magic of the silver screen, though, proved to be a disappointment to me. It was in fact we were told, nothing more than a white-washed wall! Before the screen, and within the darkness of the lower black-masking which surrounded the picture, the all important speaker was situated. The sound emitted from this insignificant-looking piece of equipment would have hardly gained approval from present-day Hi-Fi enthusiasts. Nonetheless, in a direct contradiction of statement, as it were, the 'silent' picture had its own sound — and the public loved it! Yes, *canned* music had arrived. True, this was but carefully selected 'mood music' on record, cued and rehearsed to perfection before the theatre doors were opened. But no longer did the exhibitor depend solely upon the live orchestra — or the services of a lone pianist. And just around the corner, too, so to speak, talkies were about to rear their money-spinning heads to herald the Golden Era of Talking Pictures.

At this moment, however, I noticed in the semi-darkness, a curtained recess before the screen in which were placed a piano, stool and benches with music-stands. "Ah," exclaimed our guide noticing my observations, "we still have occasions, at present, anyway," he qualified, "to call upon the good services of Miss Wetherby the leader of our little trio. There are still pictures," he elaborated, "with musical scores provided for which we are still committed." The manager had sighed meaningfully and to my father he had added in an undertone, "But not for long, I'm happy to say; for soon now we shall have talking pictures and I can pay-off my not-too-talented musicians. Yes, indeed," he went on knowingly, "soon now, silent pictures will be a thing of the past." To me, he had added encouragingly, "You've come at an opportune time, my boy."

A moment later, the manager's words still paramount in my mind, we left the hall and proceeded to the place in which I was to spend so many years of my life – the projection room.

Access to the projection room (known also as the operating box) was by means of an exterior iron stairway. I recall thinking even this must be an improvement on the vertical interior ladder I had heard about from my friends in other cinemas. Upon entering the operating box, the manager waved a hand before us and declared proudly: "These are my projection room staff."

The staff consisted of a chief projectionist, a second and third. The third operator (as we had already been enlightened by the manager) was but merely a trainee, i.e. film-rewind boy and general factotum; the situation in fact, for which I was being engaged.

The fact that the chief projectionist proved to be an ex-grammar school boy himself, I still feel impressed my father favourably. Indeed, even at this late juncture had he retained any doubts of letting me enter the picture theatre, this coincidence completely dispelled them. Furthermore, Tony Barrington, the chief, possessed undeniable charm and an ease of manner which put me immediately at ease also – and wasn't lost on my father either. Tony Barrington was a tall, thin, clean-shaven person in his early thirties.

From beneath a tattered cap he wore (for no apparent reason I thought – then) his blond hair protruded in a cluster of boyish ringlets. His lively eyes were blue and sincere and when he spoke his voice was both soft and pleasant. Yes, I liked the chief.

On the other hand, the second projectionist, Ken Dawson, (also a likeable character, but from a different background altogether, I remember thinking) struck me as an overgrown Billy Bunter of a somewhat more rugged nature. Even then as his colleague introduced my father and myself, he was busily engaged pushing a large piece of cake into his eager mouth. He turned from the small window through which he had been peering at the picture and grinned sheepishly. Pushing a flabby hand after the fast receding cake which still protruded from his thick lips, he gulped a greeting.

The manager smiled knowingly at my father before indicating the rewind room for our perusal.

As we entered the cupboard-like stuffy room, a teenager of about my own age, was carelessly rewinding films without the slightest regard for the delicate nature of the print or care required in checking for faulty joints which could well cause breakdown during projection.

Yes, possessing my own home projector had already instilled in me the care and respect required for the celluloid upon which the film makers had given so much, financially and otherwise.

Beneath the bench upon which the film was maltreated by the pale-faced slender lad with owl-like glasses, a metal cabinet was situated for storage of film not in use. Oddly enough perhaps; having repaired numerous tattered prints at home; was the overpowering smell of peardrops from the film cement used both in the make-up of convenient reels for projection and for the re-making or repair of faulty joints as required.

Back in the projection room, before the manager made his apologetic departure pointing out that his chief operator would explain 'all we wanted to know', he lingered long enough to tell us how the 'retiring' rewind-boy had scratched and ruined an entire feature film with his neglected finger-nails, dropped a 'two-reeler' into a water fire-bucket and

14

many other 'incidents' which made the proprietor feel his suitability for the post of trainee projectionist was questionable. With this said, the manager winked in our direction, then left us in the capable hands of Tony Barrington.

As briefly as possible, the operator, while dutifully engaged upon the job itself, explained the basic functions of the equipment he was handling and the general duties of the projectionist who used it.

In my ever-ready notebook, I entered there and then the following haphazard summary:

'Two projectors with Carbon-Arc, Hand-fed lighting apparatus. Low Intensity carbons used. Operation: Positive and Negative sticks 'shorted' together, then separated and maintained at correct gap for light projection. Requires constant attention as carbons burn away.

'Disc-Talkie equipment coupled with projectors, but not yet in use.

'Amplifier and non-synchronised units (for 'canned music' and 'play-out' requirements on records.)

'Change-over Device (to change from one projector to another at end and beginning of reels while maintaining continuity of picture.) Sliding Rod (with Lens Shutters) attached to wall in front of projectors. Fire Safety Shutters situated above all projection room glass apertures facing auditorium. Independent emergency release points located by each projector.

'Lantern for Slide Advertisements etc.

'Various switches for house-lighting, etc., and exterior illumination.'

This then (as far as I can remember) was the kind of hastily jotted notes — though by no means comprehensive — I recorded in my notebook on that memorable visit to The Electric Picture Theatre.

Later, in keen anticipation, I awaited the letter which would confirm my appointment and notification of starting date.

The distance between home and The Electric Picture Theatre was some twelve miles or more and as no suitable transport was available, my own means of conveyance was a vital necessity. For this purpose, my brother, Harold (a mechanical genius in his own rights), acquired for me — at bargain price, I might add, a second-hand motorcycle from a local dealer. Fully aware, not only for my safety, but that punctuality was an essential factor in my work, he meticulously over-hauled and repaired the small, yet efficient, two-stroke, belt-driven Levis motorcycle to near perfection. This was just as well, for I was to work a six-day week from ten-thirty in the morning until closedown of show at approximately the same time at night. Sunday was my day off.

On the first day of my appointment, fully equipped with the notes I had scribbled at the interview, I sat astride my flamboyantly painted machine in the impressive colours of red and yellow, and in a mood of tense anticipation, headed for the local town — and The Electric Picture Theatre.

At my destination I was in time to encounter Ken Dawson, the second operator, struggling laboriously up the iron stairway to the projection room, laden with heavy film transit cases. Stating the obvious, I remarked the cases looked heavy and could I be of assistance. The operator sighed and through his thick lips uttered something to the effect that the chief was working on a rope-and-tackle idea to enable us to pull the wretched things up.

I had nodded understandingly, and as some measure of willingness to ease the load, I bravely followed my chubby colleague with a case of 'two-reelers' in each hand. On entering the operating box, Tony Barrington turned from the projector arc-lamp he was cleaning. He proffered a broad smile of welcome, remarking it was good to see me on time and he hoped I would 'stay the course'. Then, without further formalities, he indicated on the wall a notice headed: DAILY ROUTINE PROCEDURE FOR PROJEC-TIONISTS and signed authoritatively — The Management.

The notice read:

Monday: Programme make-up. It is the responsibility of the Chief Projectionist to ensure that the complete programme has been received from the Renters. Any films missing must — repeat must

16

be reported to the manager immediately.

When required, a member of the projection staff must collect (by any means available) any films overdue at the station, if not received by normal road transport.

Note: A company bicycle is provided for this contingency.

Ensure all storage batteries for Emergency Lighting etc., are checked and maintained in a *fully-charged* condition.

Other routine duties at Chief Projectionist's discretion.

Tuesday: Routine box duties and maintenance, cleaning, etc.

Wednesday: *All* electrical equipment to be checked throughout the entire theatre by Chief and delegated operator.

Thursday: House lighting to be lowered from auditorium ceiling by Chief and cleaned by third projectionist. (It must be stressed that the cat-walk can be dangerous and must be used with extreme care.)

If no programme change, all seating must be scrutinised for loose screws and secure where necessary.

Heating and lighting (EXITS Etc.) checked and any lamp replacements to be made by third projectionist.

Friday: General duties at discretion of Chief Operator.

Saturday: *FIRE DRILL* (Procedure as directed by Management.)

Exterior lighting (still frames, etc.) to be checked and cleaned.

Chief Projectionist to ensure safe dispatch of programme.

Special Note: This notice is intended as a general guide only to the duties of projectionists and does not, by any means, exclude *any* member of the projection staff from other jobs (such as Bill-Posting, etc.) as required.

Signed,
The Manager

Tony Barrington must have noticed the expression of concern on my face and remarked in his reassuring manner, "Don't let it bother you too much, Geoffrey, it reads worse than it is. Come, let me show you around the theatre in daylight," he added with a smile, "before you give Ken, here, a hand with the programme."

As I followed the friendly figure of Barrington into the auditorium, I noticed a man on a ladder in front of the screen with a long-handled brush in one hand.

The screen, explained the chief, due to disconsolation by smoke, has to be brightened up quite frequently, you know.

I didn't and was about to put a question to the chief when an old woman, carrying a large bucket of water, staggered into view. It is strange, indeed, that even now after so many years, I still have a mental picture of that pathetic character. Her pained, tired countenance was wrinkled like a dried prune, while her fat legs must have made it difficult enough to walk, let alone work!

"Here," I had said on impulse, "let me carry that bucket for you."

At that juncture, the man on the ladder turned from the screen he was about to white-wash, and remarked crisply: "Young man, if that woman is unable to carry her own pail of water, then certainly she is unfit to work here at all. Now hurry along with the chief; I'm sure he has plenty for you to do, yourself."

I must have uttered something like 'yes, sir,' and hastened after Tony Barrington, thinking as I went 'this must be the other side of the charming person with whom I had my interview earlier.'

A short while later, I was directed into a shabby room adjacent to the proscenium labled 'Musicians and Cleaners'. Having little time to reflect on the somewhat unusual arrangement of both parties sharing the same accommodation, I experienced the rare opportunity of meeting three of the strangest people I have ever encountered at the same time.

Firstly, my companion introduced me to Miss Wetherby, a very elderly spinster with straight white hair draped close to her lean face. Immediately I noticed she experienced extreme difficulty with her steel-rimmed glasses which frequently fell from her face. The thing which intrigued me mostly about this observation was the deft manner in which the woman repeatedly caught and replaced the spectacles on her bird-like nose with almost monotonous regularity.

Then, as though in direct contrast, Joe Waldron, the trumpeter, was introduced to me. He was a short, pale-faced man with large sad eyes. He was bald, I noted, save for a monk-like ring of brown hair surrounding his cranium. He must have been, I thought, well beyond the wrong side of fifty.

Albert Meed, the violinist, for his part, was a somewhat more sturdy character, though of similar age to the trumpeter. His eyes were fish-like and he sported a mass of ungovernable grey hair. His hands, I remember, were small and constantly on the move. It was as though he feared a momentary pause in motion might render his long fingers useless for the job he had to do under the rigorous supervision of Miss Wetherby.

It was not until later during the evening performance, did I have the opportunity of assessing the musical talents of the quaint trio for myself. The manager had called me from the projection box to assist a new girl to load her sales-tray before the interval. Having done this not unpleasant chore, I entered the hall on the pretext of checking the Exit lights and nonchalantly made my way to the enclosure proudly termed the Orchestra Pit. Here, Miss Wetherby was stretching her thin neck upwards to gaze at the flickering shadows on the screen, while simultaneously playing the piano before her. With her, similarly postured, sat the other elderly musicians playing their instruments with an equal dedication to that of their devoted leader. At that moment, the scene on the screen changed to a young boy in Confederate uniform − the star of the film − who's doubtful honour to fame in the picture was to blow into his trumpet at frequent intervals to entreat help for his troops under siege. I recollect thinking if the young trooper's trumpet call had been so inadequately off-key as provided by our trumpeter, indeed, I felt the young soldier's effort would have had the adverse effect on the morale of his desperately required reinforcements!

However, it was fortunate that I had availed myself of that opportunity to witness the last of the picture theatre players at work, for that film was the last of the 'silents' to be screened at The Electric Picture Theatre. Even so, I might add, my beloved Aunt Amy, herself a one-time violinist in a picture theatre, would charm me into nostalgia in later years with her delightful repertoire of music from the early movies.

However, to return to Miss Wetherby and her picture-house players; the sad day arrived when the pathetic little group were paid off by the management. With a Buster Keaton expression on his tired face, the trumpeter, followed by the dishevelled figure of the violinist, left the theatre. Miss Wetherby, her lips trembling, followed shortly after them. In a sense, the departure of those lovable characters marked — for me anyway — the end of an era for which I still consider myself fortunate to have experienced, if but for such a brief duration.

The following week after the 'last of the silents' had been unceremoniously returned to the renters, the projection room of the Electric Picture Theatre became virtually a nest of sound engineers and company technicians. The disc-talkie equipment which had remained silent for so long, was at last brought to life by the skilful hands of those early engineers who's keen dedication to their task opened the picture house doors to the Golden Era of Talking Pictures.

For all that, with the arrival of the eagerly awaited talking pictures came a renewed responsibility for the projectionist which rested heavily upon his shoulders. For example, a film break was no longer a simple matter. For now should there be a break in the film, not only would the sound be lost for that reel, but for every small piece of film removed when effecting repair, the projectionist had to ensure the *exact* replacement — in blank celluloid — was inserted into the film in order to maintain synchronisation with the record on projection. It was not easy. Moreover, regardless of film breaks, the slightest accident with the record pick-up during projection would mean either the projectionist missed that reel (switching to the other projector) or *re-starting* the 'lost' reel again! One can well imagine audience reaction

20

to such unfortunate circumstances.

I squirm at the memory of the time when I was obliged to repair a Viennese musical epic in my early days associated with S.O.D. (Sound On Disc). The film, when later projected, though maintaining synchronisation, was like viewing TV today and momentarily losing the picture every few minutes!

There were, of course, even greater technical problems to be encountered in those early days of disc-talkies, but by the very nature of these memoirs, the only technical reference I use in this book is merely to emphasise a situation. Other technical data not required for this purpose will be omitted intentionally.

This point established, then; I turn now to the simultaneous new purge in publicity surrounding those glamorous, though hectic days when every exhibitor in the country raced to get on the talkie band-wagon ahead of his rival.

Well I remember the day when the 'big' man himself summoned us to his office; then as though planning a major military exercise, briefed us on the importance of greater originality in publicity if we were to successfully compete with the other picture theatres in town. It behoved us all to come up with an idea, he insisted. While he accepted the normal publicity channels as 'useful' and agreed an extension of the range for bill-posting, leaflet-posting, press coverage, etc., was very necessary, none-the-less, this in itself was still not enough. What he required was really good, *original*, publicity stunts which would catch the public eye and subsequently their cash at the box-office.

One opposition house, I remember, had already ventured bravely into this new advertising technique. But alas, their first effort, the idea of one of the theatre staff 'doing the town' in full cowboy regalia on a nondescript horse, sadly misfired due to a group of astute schoolboys. For on the back of the unfortunate rider was a placard which read: 'I'm the man who cleans up the West. See me tonight in action at The Palace'. On recognising the 'Westerner' the lively lads from the local school, surrounded by a crowd of midday shoppers, yelled unkindly: 'You're not, you know. You are the one who cleans up the picture theatre.'

It was a very demoralised 'Westerner' who rode off into

the sunset.

But if the publicity *faux pas* of the Palace staff proved so disappointing, I hate to reflect on the possible results of some of the ideas put forward by our little group that day in the manager's office, had they been put to the test. For instance, Ken Dawson suggested we too, could do a Western stunt if more suitably disguised than the unfortunate man from the Palace. Only we could do one better — we could hold up the local bank! I hasten to add, this suggestion was immediately vetoed as indeed the idea to have a shapely usherette perform the Dance of the Seven Veils twice nightly in the foyer to publicise our forthcoming musical extravaganza. On the more modest scale, however, an idea of mine concerning bill-posting on certain hoardings, was accepted; mainly because I believe, there was little further cost involved — and it was simple. All the bill-poster did was to paste his publicity material on the hoardings upside down, with a sticker (the correct way up) which read: 'Whichever way you look at this picture it is sensational! Don't miss it.'

The stunt worked all right, yet I still have no recollection of receiving due credit for the idea. However, I soon became aware of a renewed respect from the theatre staff and was no longer referred to as 'the lad'.

I do know though, I dreaded the occasions when I was called upon to assist the doorman-cum-assistant-manager on his routine door-to-door leaflet and special poster 'raids' into the surrounding district. He would sit astride his absolutely filthy motorcycle with sidecar attached in which I sat surrounded by thousands of leaflets, posters — and a large bucket of paste. This messy adhesive would spray over me with uncomfortable regularity as this madman rounded corners on two wheels, the sidecar in the air! I honestly believe this diabolical character was once a pilot in The Royal Flying Corp before joining us at the picture theatre. How I ever survived those hair-raising excursions with that reckless man bent low over the handlebars of his infernal machine, I shall never know. I do know though, I could 'paper' an entire street while he was chatting up the young housewives in another. Alas, I was very young at the time.

22

Apart from my bill-posting activities, I think on reflection, my introduction to assistant stoker and seat repairer duties were even worse than my perilous trips in that wretched sidecar. Although the doorman-cum-assistant-manager would normally throw his hand in, so to speak, with the heating arrangements of the theatre, I was detailed to maintain the temperature of the theatre boiler at a constant level as determined by the management. At various intervals during my duties in the projection room, I would be 'allowed' to proceed to the stoke-hole, stoke up as required and then unobtrusively enter the auditorium to check the radiators. Airlocks in radiators, I was informed, were both a source of danger and a potential irritation to the patrons should they start 'knocking'. With the appropriate key clutched authoritatively in my hand, it behoved me to 'bleed' any such radiator by releasing the trapped air; a not too pleasant task at any time, but in the dark with a boiling radiator 'dancing' at my elbow, I assure you, even less desirable.

The periodical seat check, on the other hand, was usually a chore in which all the male staff were employed. And believe me, the seating provided in theatres in those early days, left much to be desired. For instance, the first four rows of seating nearest the screen — in this particular cinema, anyway — were nothing more elaborate than ordinary benches screwed to the floor. And although our picture-house proudly advertised seating accommodation as second-to-none in town, I hate to think in retrospect what kind of seating was provided by other theatres in the area! Anyway, while I am happy to relate vandalism was something we seldom experienced in the theatre in those days, we would none-the-less have something in the region of a hundred seats a week to repair. True this figure included the replacement of loose back-rests, elbow-rests, seats and sometimes even broken seat standards (when the picture was particularly exciting) but quite frankly, whatever the figure, a routine task I personally could well have done without. Indeed, perhaps for this very reason, whenever I visit a theatre these days, I give you my word, I treat my seat with the greatest of respect! While on the subject of seats, I feel I must mention the occasion when following our nightly seat-check after the theatre closed, for any possible unextinguished cigarette ends which might cause a fire, I found something quite different — a bundle of one hundred pound notes! The following day I learnt this money I had handed in had been claimed by a local farmer. I was also informed the recipient had been hard pushed to even express his thanks for the return of the money he had drawn earlier from the bank to pay off his fruit pickers the next day.

These early episodes then, of my association with The Electric Picture Theatre are perhaps not the most important during my first years with the cinema, but for no logical reason I can think of at the moment, come to mind above all else during that period. However, by the time gossip had come through the 'grapevine' of the introduction to certain picturedromes throughout the country of a magnificent new attraction to the theatres — the Cinema Organ, I felt I had successfully 'stayed the course' of my initial training at the picture-house. Moreover, the exciting news that the film industry was rapidly approaching the 'crest of the wave' with subsequent new super picture theatres hastily being built, not to mention the further acquisition of disused buildings such as old chaples and the like, for conversion into dependently promoted theatres, was no insignificant fillip to my ego; I felt I was at last, truly on the way! And indeed, why not? For the projectionist was now more than ever in great demand by old and new exhibitors alike — and at that time I had been upgraded to the proud rank of Second Projectionist, Ken Dawson having already left for richer pastures.

In all this, however, I make no apology for saying the most significant news (as far as I was concerned) in those wonderful cinematic days was the announcement by my younger brother, Gordon, that he, too, was about to enter the cinema industry.

Strangely enough, if I may digress for a moment, although I was unaware of it then; later, fate would have it that most of my life in the cinema was destined to be in company with my brother, Gordon — a privilege indeed. For Gordon's tireless dedication to the cinema, his wit, and constant regard for his fellow workers, was, and always will be, an

24

inspiration to me. For not only did he serve the world of cinema in peacetime, but carried his dedication for the picture show across the war-torn battlefields of Europe, while serving with a Mobile Film Unit in World War II.

But back in The Electric Picture Theatre at this time however, I was becoming uncomfortably aware of something which for so long, I refused to accept — the nagging belief in the back of my mind that the 'big' man, by exploiting the code of the theatre, that 'come what may, the show must go on' was using this otherwise commendable maxim, to extract from his loyal employees extra duties far beyond the normal requirements of picture theatre staff. I was aware too, that Tony Barrington, the Chief, through sheer fatigue from extraneous chores, experienced extreme difficulty in keeping awake at the projector during the late evening performances. I too, for the very same reason, would sometimes nod off and let the 'unforgivable' happen — exhibit the tail-end of a reel and a 'white sheet' (screen) by missing a change-over to the other projector. In fact, it was during one of Barrington's bouts of drowsiness one night that he had a film break in his projector — and I promptly learnt why the projectionist in those days invariably wore a cap! Startled into immediate action by a tongue of flame as the film ignited in the picture gate, my colleague snatched his tattered cap smartly from his blond head and snuffed out the flame as he closed down the projector. With a quick smile and a nod from the Chief, I opened up immediately on my projector. The show went on. What might well have been a disaster in any other similar circumstances, was averted by the skilful hands of this tired projectionist, and his dedication to his public. Yes, a good lad was Barrington — one of the old school. I also remember, by the way, that the following day I too, aquired a suitable cap for myself.

On the humorous side at this juncture, however, there was the occasion when, as part of my normal duties, I was entrusted with the mundane task of opening and closing the tabs (curtains) at the commencement and end of the performance. Not having at that time reached the luxury of electrically controlled tabs, it required someone to pull a

25

b

rope for this purpose; usually a projectionist or occasionally someone from 'the front of the house' staff.

Anyway, following a particularly tiresome day bill-posting, seat-repairing, etc., I reached the wooden box upon which the 'operator' sat at the side of the screen to await the fade-out of the picture in order to close the tabs on THE END, and unwittingly put my head in my hands. The next thing I remembered was still sitting in 'the man thinking' posture — with the house lights full up! I had fallen fast asleep.

Ironically enough perhaps, this humorous though somewhat humiliating experience in full view of the departing picture theatre patrons, had a good side effect. As providence would have it, a director of the company happened to be in the auditorium at the time of the incident, and I learnt later, the 'big' man, himself, was suitably reprimanded for pushing his staff too much when operators were in such demand throughout the country.

It was some months later, however, that something happened at the picture-house which caused me to feel my life in that particular theatre would never be the same — Tony Barrington had decided to leave. On looking back now, I believe even then, I sensed this was inevitable sooner or later, but refused to accept the fact. For in latter months I had noticed that my colleague had become somewhat morose and decidedly out of character. I know for certain I missed his hitherto lighthearted quips and cheerful smile. Frankly, had I been a little older — and wiser at the time and not so wrapped up in my own world of celluloid, so to speak, I might have seen 'the writing on the wall'. For shortly after I had joined the picture theatre, Tony Barrington had wed a pretty young girl from the local gown shop. It was quite a quick affair, too, and quite honestly, the only significant thing I remember of the occasion, was the unpalatable chunk of cake with which Tony presented Ken Dawson and myself upon his return to work following a mere two-day honeymoon, this being all the time he was permitted by the management.

Unhappily, it came to my knowledge later, Tony's young, impressionable spouse, was as keenly attracted to the

26

masculine frivolity of the local dance-hall as her husband was dedicated to the cinema. Emotionally, something had to happen, I can see it now — and it did.

I clearly remember the night when I went to the rear of the theatre after the show, to collect my motorcycle, and unbeknown to Tony and his wife, unwittingly overheard the bitter discourse between them as Barrington fetched his bicycle from the shed-racks. Even now I can recall the irate voice of Barrington's wife in heated debate. I went home that night both sad and disillusioned: surely this awful thing couldn't happen to someone as kind and understanding as Tony Barrington?

"You know, Geoffrey," Tony had solemnly confided to me later, "there comes a time when one must decide for oneself that which is most important in life. While it is true I shall, in all probability, miss the cinema, I am certain I would miss my wife more, you understand?"

I think I did.

"You see," Tony had felt obliged to elaborate, "that is yet another sacrifice one must make if dedicated to the projection room — the loss of normal social existence outside the theatre. For let us be quite frank about this, Geoffrey," he had gone on, "by the very nature of the job, we work while others play."

Barrington must have noticed the forlorn expression on my face, for he quickly qualified: "For a single person, like yourself, you deprive no one *but* yourself of the accepted social way of life. But with someone else to consider" — he had forced that fetching smile of his — "it is a different matter altogether. You follow me?"

I did indeed; but said nothing. For how can one tell a friend that he knows damn well that a marriage was about to break up if that person was not around to keep an eye on his irresponsible wife and the other men with whom she openly flirted at the local dance-halls!

On reflection, yes, I am sure that Tony Barrington made the only decision he could in the circumstances, in order to try and save his marriage. Ironically enough though, this wasn't to be, for the last I heard of Tony Barrington and his fickle wife, was of their separation.

27

As I turn from this unhappy episode, I feel no excuse on my part is necessary, however, for the somewhat lengthy revelations of the 'Barrington affair'. Like my dear friend said, this is an integral part of the sacrifice the projectionist is expected to make as he dedicates himself to the cinema, and cannot, therefore, be excluded from this narrative.

It was at the time of Tony's untimely departure from the cinema, that my brother, Gordon, was engaged as assistant projectionist at The Palace Cinema in another town. At the same time, this small, independent company was looking for projectionists to run another theatre – The Hippodrome. I was interested. But frankly, had Tony Barrington still been with me, I am almost certain that in spite of the prospect of a considerable increase in wages, and working in the same town as my brother, I might well have stayed longer at The Electric Picture Theatre. But now, with Tony Barrington's departure, another thing happened to make up my mind.

Although by that time I was an 'advanced' teenager, the fact is the 'big' man had put another, less qualified, yet older projectionist in charge of the box when Tony left; this in itself, would not have been instrumental in my leaving that cinema. No, the truth was, I suppose, I had lost complete faith in the man who had engaged me but a few years earlier, and I still feel not without some justification. Having parted company with Tony Barrington was bad enough, but to find a deceitful trait in the character of the person for whom I had previously held in such high esteem, must have been the deciding factor for my resignation from that theatre. I think, perhaps, I saw my employer for what he really was, following a rumpus one day with a member of his staff. I asked Tony later, if the manager felt so strongly about the incident, why had he not dismissed the person he claimed responsible for the alleged misdemeanour? I remember the odd smirk I received from my companion. "Geoffrey, my boy," Tony had sighed heavily, "Not only does our boss live by the code of the theatre – he has one of his own, too."

"Oh," I had responded simply as Tony Barrington tapped the side of his long nose significantly.

"Oh yes, indeed," Tony clarified wryly, "simply this;

'Never sack a member of your staff; create a position whereby that person is *glad* to sack himself. That way, it looks better at Head Office, you know," Barrington had concluded.

In short, all this then, taken into consideration, must have been the reason why I applied for the post of Second Projectionist at The Hippodrome — and got it.

As I write this next sequence, I recall someone once said: 'For Heaven's sake, surround me with fat men' (or something like that), well my new employer, by no stretch of the imagination could be classified as anything but just that — a very fat man indeed. He loved both money and women, and I think perhaps in that order too! Moreover, he made no attempt to hide the fact, either. I liked this man for his sincerity and understanding for those around him. Equally likeable, was the charming auburn-haired girl with whom he shared his apartment above the cinema. Indeed, at that time, a goddess in my eyes, too. This man also lived by a code. In fact, a very old maxim of true show people, which meant simply: 'Be nice to your friends on the way up, you might well meet them again on the way down!'

Yes, my new boss had much of the charm of Tony Barrington, but without the perfunctory moral etiquette of that time, which had been instilled in both Tony Barrington and myself. Certainly, to refer to this astonishing showman as Bohemian, however, would have been an understatement; he simply took convention by the scruff of the neck and threw it to the wind!

To enlarge on this singular character, I could do worse than relate the occasion when — assuming his office vacant — I raced into the room to collect some P.R.S. forms (Performing Rights Society) one night, only to find this corpulent gentleman in tight embrace with an amorous blonde. Nonchalantly, he winked over the girl's shoulder in my direction as unconsciously I returned a similar optical reflex, and hastily returned to the projection room.

Odd though, now I come to think about it, that my new employer should have had so many romantic interludes from time to time, yet I have no recollection of this man's auburn-haired companion raising any objection. To believe the 'Goddess' had no knowledge of her partner's romantic adventures

29

with other women would, to say the least, be extremely silly. On the other hand, I can think of no time when this beautiful woman was in any way similarly compromised with other men in the theatre. Strange. If unbeknown to me and others in the cinema, the 'Goddess' *had* been involved with other men, well, all I can say is she must have been the ultimate in cunning deceit.

I do know though, (as I have already suggested) I personally, was becoming acutely aware I was finding this fascinating woman distinctly disturbing. Frankly, there were the times when I found myself viewing the 'Goddess' with something more than youthful admiration. Ever present in her beautiful eyes was the expression of one about to be kissed, which I have to admit I found painfully difficult to resist in spite of the absurdity of the situation. A trivial thing to remember, perhaps. But is it not true, it is the seemingly insignificant things in life one mentally recaptures in later years, while events of greater moment pass beyond recall. Insignificant or otherwise, I feel nevertheless justified in relating the incident when this auburn-haired temptress requested my assistance one night, to rectify an electrical fault in her apartment.

A few moments later, climbing on a chair, her enticing figure seductively silhouetted by the light from the adjacent room, I was told there had been a flash from the light-fitting as the lamp was switched on. "Can you fix it for me, Geoffrey?" she had asked in a tone of voice that had thrilled me.

I can not recall how long it was before I was able to answer her query. The only thing I knew for certain at that moment, was an irresistible urge to feel the close proximity of that beautiful creature's body against mine. Yes, I was growing up fast, and like Tony Barrington had correctly predicted, already I was missing the normal contact with girls outside the theatre. It was disturbing, to say the least.

"Geoffrey," the voice had come through to me at length, "do you intend me to stand up here like this all night, or are you going to help me?"

Somehow or other I found my voice and with suitable apology for my indifferent behaviour, soon rectified the fault for which I had been called to the room.

On leaving, I was rewarded far in excess of my wildest hopes. Not only did the 'Goddess' praise me for my electrical expertise, but paused long enough to kiss me firmly on my left cheek. "Thank you, dear boy," she had chanted, her dreamy eyes searching my reddened countenance. "You will help me again, sometime, yes?"

"Yes madam," I had returned, becoming suddenly aware of my somewhat junior status in the cinema. "Anytime."

My face must have remained flushed upon my return to the projection room, for my new associate turned from the projector he was attending and enquired jokingly: "How did you like the Garden of Eden?"

"The Garden of Eden?" I had put back lamely.

"Come off it, Geoffrey," my good natured companion had flung back at me. "Everyone in the theatre refers to the apartment as 'The Garden of Eden': I thought you knew that."

It was a timely change-over, however, which prevented any possible rejoinder on my part.

Frankly, (and that is the only way it is going to be in this outspoken book) from that precise moment onwards, I realised if I were to stay in the cinema, I would have to satisfy my natural desires for the opposite sex within the four walls in which I spent so much of my life. Unless of course, I did a Tony Barrington; got married and left the world of the cinema far behind me. At that time, however, any such notion was completely out of the question. My first love then was decidedly in favour of the cinema. If, on the other hand, I could find some measure of compensation without departing from my fanatical resolve to work in a picture-house — so much the better!

Thus resolved, my mind turned (perhaps naturally enough) to the recent addition to our theatre staff: a voluptuous blonde usherette, with whom I had good reason to believe there would be little opposition to the occasional kiss and cuddle in the semi-darkness of the cinema. Unfortunately, in my eagerness to make contact, so to speak, with this stimulating creature, I fear I let my normal discretion go by the board, with almost humiliating results.

31

During my routine 'breather' from the operating box one night, I entered the rear of the hall where I knew Diana, the new usherette would be standing with her confectionery tray held below her ample bust in readiness for the interval. Playfully coming up behind the girl, I slipped my hands around her, and between the buttons of her uniform to sense the contour of her delicate bust. "Guess who?" I whispered.

"The King of Siam," she hissed back at me. "And if you don't remove your nasty little paws immediately, I'll bash 'em with my torch."

I remember saying something facetious like; "That would be like hitting your face to get rid of a fly, wouldn't it?"

Before the girl could respond, the curtains behind us separated and my employer ambled into the auditorium. Hastily I made to withdraw my hands from within the blonde's uniform, only to find my left cuff caught on a hook in the interior cloth! The big man, his hands clenched characteristically behind his massive back, came purposefully towards us. A moment later he paused at my side to gaze indifferently at the screen. Then, without turning his head, he cocked his right eyebrow and remarked quietly: "What are you doing here, Geoffrey?"

I had my answer ready. "Just popped in for some cigarettes," I shot back.

My kindly employer proffered an odd smile as he turned to leave. "Indeed, well you won't find them there," he whispered in my left ear. "Now get back to the box, there's a good chap."

This then, was the type of man for whom I was fortunate to work at that time. That regrettable incident with Diana, with all its potential implications, could well have meant my untimely departure from the cinema, but for the complete understanding of that worldly gentleman. From then on, therefore, I made it my business not to embarrass my employer with any similar reiteration of that nature. The fact that my employer's example in this respect left much to be desired, was completely irrelevant; he was, after all, my boss — and the King can do no wrong!

As far as Diana was concerned, however, she too, conducted herself with impeccable decorum within the precincts of the cinema. On the other hand, what we did with our limited time outside the theatre, was a very different matter altogether. Indeed, a strange kind of relationship and understanding had developed between us. It was as though, she too, longed for the natural companionship of the opposite sex while 'imprisoned' nightly at her place of employment. "But," she had insisted, "with no strings attached." This suited me fine, of course. After all, the 'arrangement' was precisely what I had in mind myself at that juncture. However, the time came when, perhaps sooner than I expected, I was ready to forsake such irresponsible resolutions, and indeed a lot more, too, in order to induce my tantalising companion to behave more 'freely' towards me. Hitherto, this lovely girl had used her abundant charm to keep me almost literally at arms length, since the 'cuff caper', with all the dexterous sophistication of one many years her senior. Whenever our relationship was in danger of getting out of hand, Diana would look at me with a hurt expression of disenchantment, like a child who has just been told there was no Father Christmas. With this look of strange sadness in her misty blue eyes, she would immediately counter-attack by asking me to explain the functions of cinema technique, etc. Before I realised it, I had forgotten my seductive inclinations, inflicting upon my companion instead, a barrage of trite technical data from the projection room. Yes, Diana was smart all right, and when cornered, used the strength of my other 'love' in self-defence. But on the never-to-be-forgotten day I took Diana to the seaside in my Austin Chubby (another acquisition by my brother Harold) I knew I would have to fight desperately the disquieting desire to have the complete love of the beautiful blonde at my side. I realised, of course, only too well, the full significance of the irrevocable action I had in mind, should I succumb to the reckless compulsion to have sexual intercourse with Diana. I was also aware, of course, of what this would mean to Diana and her family, not to mention my own folk. But alas, passion has but little reason, has it not? None-the-less, the fact that my parents graciously conceded to let me lower the status of the family by working in 'halls of iniquity' at such an early age, was one thing; but to have a son who betrayed a young girl's affection by lustful misbehaviour, would have been nothing short of monstrous and quite unforgivable. And who could argue with that? Certainly I couldn't. For all that, the nagging sensation within me persisted as I parked the little car in the secluded sand dunes by the sea, and in the heat of the day, commenced to make love.

I remember, of all things, the large, floppy, white hat Diana threw aside with a devil-may-care gesture as she proceeded to unbutton her cheap print dress to reveal the full beauty of her firm breasts, protected only by a skin-tight blue bathing costume. I might have known, though, she had merely intended to tease me; yes, even before she giggled knowingly at the disappointment on my face. Regardless of this, however, I manoeuvred feverishly to try and release that flimsy garment, held tightly by those wretched neck straps − but to no avail. Cleverly, as always, Diana played her vital cards to perfection. Separating herself momentarily from my passionate overtures, she divulged a dampness around her eyes, perhaps a touch of fear and disgust too: I'm not sure now. I do know however, I could never take advantage of any women with such an expression of sadness and utter disbelief for what might befall her in a moment of illicit ecstasy.

"Geoffrey," Diana had sighed heavily, "accepting I'm not much of a catch, believe me, dear, I'm still what is generally known as a good girl." She had wrinkled her upturned nose. "And if it is all the same to you, I would like to keep it that way."

"Then you don't intend to get married?" I had flung back foolishly.

"You silly boy," Diana had countered tickling me beneath the chin, "all I am saying is; that if any man wants me − completely, it will have to be through a church doorway, that's all." She shrugged, I remember her adding: "Otherwise I would prefer to finish my days a virgin − if it's all the same to you." The tears came then as she concluded chokingly: "You do understand, don't you Geoffrey?"

I did, and told her the sooner we found that church doorway, the better. And never since have I held anyone in higher esteem than that seductive blonde usherette from a humble background. Whether I might have married Diana eventually, honestly I cannot say; for it was shortly following our exotic excursion to the seaside, the sad news reached me one night as I prepared a projector with film, that Diana had been killed in a road accident on the way to the cinema.

I know I was stunned into silence for a while, before I made an excuse to my senior colleague that I had to check the theatre boiler. He had nodded, turning away understandingly to allow me to proceed to the stoke-hole, where, thanking God I had let Diana go a virgin, I cried for a very long time.

For some time after this unhappy episode, whenever I had occasion to enter the rear of the auditorium, I imagined I could still see Diana with her well-laden tray held dutifully before her, only to find instead, a hard-faced individual, with whom I found the briefest dialogue an unpleasant chore. Yes, I missed Diana in more ways than one. In fact, not only had my family noticed the somewhat morose change in my attitude in the ensuing months following the untimely loss of my girl friend, but so had someone else – the 'Goddess'.

It was immediately after the close-down of the show one night, that the 'Goddess' approached me in the foyer as I was about to leave. "If you're not in a hurry to get home, Geoffrey, she had opened up in that alluring voice of hers, "I wonder if you could spare me a few moments?"

Though apprehensive for what this beautiful woman might need me at such a late hour, I nevertheless experienced an odd sensation of elation; for no one so exquisite as my employer's companion, could possibly require me for anything but to my advantage.

"I'm in no hurry," I assured her with what I considered an adult nonchalant air, then followed the 'Goddess' to her apartment, where too, I had expected to see my boss. It was with no little satisfaction I learnt the gentleman was at one of his other cinemas. Why I should have felt like this, frankly I don't know; for since the tragic loss of Diana, my more basic inclinations had suffered a considerable set-back. While hitherto I had a singular physical desire towards the 'Goddess'; for no logical reason I could think of on this occasion, it no longer existed. But let me hasten to confess, however, I still observed this remarkable person with something more than normal appreciation for one so beautiful. No, the truth was, I suppose, I was still emotionally disturbed, having lost Diana so tragically, leaving a void where once the uninhibited passion of youth knew no bounds.

The 'Goddess' had sat studying her carefully manicured hands for a moment, before she turned to me with a trace of a pained expression in her lovely eyes. "Geoffrey," she said with an undertone of resignation, "I have taken it unto myself to ask you here, alone, to discuss a personal matter with you." She had forced one of her divine smiles. "But I hasten to assure you, if you think for one moment, Geoffrey, I have no right to involve myself in your private affairs, please do not hesitate to tell me so. For indeed, you could be right."

I remember sighing, and desperately wishing my beautiful companion would come to the point. But the fact that anyone, least of all, the 'Goddess' would go to such lengths to even discuss my personal interests, whatever they might be, must have inflated my ego considerably, for I responded immediately. "Please," I said rather pompously, "feel free to speak your mind. I find your interest in my welfare most gratifying."

"In that case," reciprocated my companion with obvious relief, "I'll come straight to the point. While I am fully aware of what the recent loss of your girl friend must mean to you, Geoffrey, you mustn't let this unhappy event in your life, put you out completely, if you know what I mean." She smiled again reassuringly. "Remember, you still have your whole life before you." I recall her deep intake of breath before she added: "And believe me, all the mourning in the world will not bring back that unfortunate girl: you must face up to this fact, Geoffrey, and the sooner the better, you understand?"

I nodded mechanically, though even then realising how easy it is to tell another what to do, when one is not in a similar unfortunate position oneself. But if the King can do no wrong, neither could the 'Goddess' as far as I was concerned. Moreover, I was deeply flattered by her concern for me, though somewhat resentful of being told how to conduct my own life – yes, even by the 'Goddess'.

Time, it is said, is a wonderful healer. So, I suppose (to some extent, anyway) is hard work. At least, I considered myself fortunate that following my intimate tête-á-tête with the 'Goddess', events transpired so quickly within the orbit of the cinematic world, I had little time to reflect on the past, and indeed, as the 'Goddess' had pointed out: It behoved me to look to the future. So that was that.

Happily for the man in the box at this time, S.O.D. (Sound on Disc) was at last on the way out. The exciting era of S.O.F. (Sound on Film) had arrived. Though perhaps ironically enough, however, any jubilation that might have been expressed by exhibitors, was to some degree offset by a new challenge yet to be confronted – the iminent approach of the big circuit cinemas. And for me too, it was unhappy news, for the possibility of my eventual acquisition of a cinema of my own, was then virtually denied in view of this new development. With untold resources behind them, the celluloid giants in the background, were a real threat to the small exhibitor, for whom, until this time, there had been but little opposition, save for the 'other picture-house down the street'.

Prompted, therefore, by this disconcerting new development, my boss immediately endeavoured to acquire sites in other major towns before they were claimed by the impending major circuits. In almost every town and city at this time, one would see the site notices which read simply: 'Site for New Super Cinema'. It was also true, it should be mentioned, that not only were these sites snatched up by the 'giants' to come, but alas, by independent and smaller groups, too, striving to stay in business. Indeed, many sites were 'held' by certain exhibitors, merely to prevent their acquisition by the big circuits as they threatened to sweep the country. Eventually, however, these 'reserved' sites, too, were taken over as the small independent theatres were devoured by the picture-house 'giants'.

Soon we were to witness the arrival of the classic circuits

known as Odeon, Gaumont-British and ABC, after the earlier enterprising circuits such as Union County Cinemas, P T C and General Theatre Corporation, etc., had been swallowed up by their adversaries. But all this was yet to come. At this juncture, however, the independent proprietors had no intention of going under without a fight. This meant, of course, a complete change in the attitude of these show-men. No longer could the indifferent exhibitor get away with an inferior house; he had to have the best in both men and equipment — and the projectionist knew it. Though tradition-ally always willing to help out in other areas when necessary; no longer would the operator tolerate the role of general factotum. Belatedly, the man in the box had gained a well-deserved new status. He had become a technician in his own right, with more positions to be filled than projectionists to meet them.

This then, was yet another memorial milestone in the progression of picture theatre entertainment: a new deal for the hitherto underrated projectionist — the man in the box.

SECTION TWO

THE GOLDEN ERA OF SOUND ON FILM

It was soon after the introduction of sound on film that I became aware the luxury super cinema, hastily being built in close proximity to the theatre in which I then worked, was not, after all, one of the new big circuit concerns — but one of our own! I was delighted. With a singular sense of pride, I would make a weekly 'inspection' of this super picture house, whenever the opportunity presented itself. It wasn't long before I became awe-inspired by the large amount of equipment being installed in this new theatre, not to mention a massive stage with all the necessary allied equipment and dressing rooms. I remember too, an impressive crude-oil engine, which I was informed could develop up to 75 h.p. under load, making the theatre electrically self-supporting in respect of both picture and theatrical presentations as required. In the projection room, I found the very latest projectors, amplifier units and theatre lighting apparatus. The latter item being a bulky contraption of numerous levers and wheels to provide every conceivable colour-mix by deft manipulation of the operator. Returning to the stage end of the theatre, I recall the large screen was mounted on rollers to enable this to be transported to the rear of the stage when not in use. In all, a very comprehensive set-up. Neither had the carefully considered decor of the theatre been overlooked, for the entire interior was later tastefully finished in delicate Autumn tints with 'comb' designs on all predominate walls as suggested by the 'Goddess'. Indeed, it *was* a pretty sight.

Yes, it was quite obvious to me even then, as young as I was, that my enterprising employer had no intention of being

39

left behind when the giant circuits reared their devouring heads. Indeed, this magnificent picture theatre proved not only to be the talk of the town, but of the rural population for miles around. It was most gratifying. Even so, I still feel had there been some restraint in expenditure in certain less vital areas, at that time, there might have been enough left in the 'kitty' to incorporate one of the rare stupendous additions to any super cinema — the cinema organ.

I do know, however, that following information in a trade paper, my brother Gordon and I made ourselves available at the first possible opportunity to visit an opposition picture house in which an early organ had been installed.

I shall never forget the thrill and enchantment Gordon and I experienced in that theatre as the tabs closed and the house lights came up; followed, a moment later, by a multi-coloured, crystal-like melodious monster from beneath the floor, upon which sat a neat little man, his left leg dancing while experienced hands deftly oscillated between alternate levels of keyboard. Certainly I have never lost the excitement of that wonderful moment and thanks to such people as Tony Moss, Robin Richmond and many other cinema celebrities keenly associated with the Cinema Organ Society of today, I can still indulge in the singular nostalgic sound of this magnificent instrument.

However, what our new cinema lacked organ-wise, to some extent anyway, I must admit was compensated by the discerning selection of pictures my astute employer had lined up for his new cinema — and especially for the opening.

It was during a brief encounter with my brother Gordon one morning at the Palace, when we were discussing the imminent opening of the Roxy and lack of projection staff, when we were approached by our employer. He ambled towards us, stuck a king-sized cigar in his mouth and without any preamble whatsoever, said suddenly: "I would like you, Gordon and Geoffrey, to assist the Chief operator in the opening of the Roxy. You will find your wages suitably increased in line with your additional responsibilities. Before we could express our appreciation and deep satisfaction for such an honour, he went on: "Your old positions have been filled. I wish you both good luck in your new theatre." With that, his hands held tightly behind his back, he swung round and sauntered away in a cloud of acrid cigar smoke.

To celebrate the exciting news of our promotions, my brother and I decided on another visit to the cinema with the organ. Indisputably we were not alone in our almost fanatical appreciation of this new sound. The interest in this latest addition to the cinema spread far and wide, bringing into the theatre hitherto non-cinema-goers for whom the cinema organ was the main attraction. Unfortunately, on this occasion, the resident organist was indisposed, his place having been taken by a younger man, for whom the bottle held an equal appeal to the valuable organ upon which he exhibited himself. Even before the feature film finished, a resounding blast of the pipe music filled the theatre as the organist came slowly into view. For a terrifying moment it seemed the intoxicated deputy had lost not only control of the console, but his ability even to stay with the organ. Swaying alarmingly from side to side, the movement inter-jected with unmentionable gesticulations as the spotlight picked him out, this substitute organist miraculously managed to survive the interlude.

Funnily enough however, he was well received by the audience who undoubtedly believed this exhibition was a deliberate comic stunt by the none-the-less talented organist with a natural flair for slapstick humour. In fact this almost perpetually inebriated musician was subsequently billed as the 'Eccentric Organist' and acclaimed by many as both a comedian and organist of distinction. Such is show business.

On the more serious side, my brother and I became very much aware that with the improvement of theatres, the equipment and indeed superior staff, a definite wind of change was imminent in cinema management technique. With the approach of the giant circuits, no longer would cinema owners tolerate the somewhat carefree set-up which existed in the earlier days of the picture theatre. A strict reorganisation was speedily being introduced throughout the entire cinema world in old and new theatres alike; with it a rigid code of discipline was impending with all the irksome rules and regulations to embrace both 'front of house' staff and all projection room employees.

41

In retaliation, as it were, the desirability of Union recognition was being equally hastily promoted with no little concern by men of foresight to protect possible intimidation of employees by unscrupulous theatre management. Soon we were to see a realistic wage structure for all grades of cinema employees, not least the projectionist with the added technical responsibility and skill required to put over a show equal to none, in the challenging era of talking pictures. Be that as it may, I still maintain there is much to be desired with regard to working conditions of cinema employees. Indeed, in many ways there has been a complete reversal of improved conditions so laboriously gained over the years, and I certainly intend to elaborate on this theme later in the book.

But to return to the Roxy. On reflection I can understand now why my employer had my brother and I transferred to this new super cinema to assist the Chief projectionist. The kindest thing I can say about this tired, slightly decrepit operator, is that he had worked so hard throughout his life in the cinema, the poor chap was virtually spent out! His health being uncertain, his reliability questionable, he needed all the help he could get. For example, there was the incident when having filled the auxiliary fuel tank to supply the theatre's engine, he left the cinema forgetting to turn off the main fuel supply tap. This resulted in an obnoxious smell of hot crude-oil filling the theatre as the engine room became flooded and the power-plant ceased to function. Fortunately, we were able to control the oil-flow from spreading to the auditorium until the arrival of the fire service who quickly dealt with the unfortunate mishap. Happily, in the meantime, we were able to switch over to the town electric supply to continue the show. A somewhat disconcerting situation for two young men with a virgin super cinema in their charge. Similary, the Chief's carelessness was equally responsible for wrecking a new projector one night, while foolishly endeavouring to gain lost time on an incorrectly scheduled programme. The projector's motors of that time were of the constant speed variety and decidedly adequate for the purpose for which they were intended, but nothing more. However, our tired projectionist felt he could well make up lost time by hand-winding the projector at a higher speed than the motor provided! Not only did this silly action have a disharmonious effect on the sound, but it was also a highly dangerous thing to do. Regardless of the caution delicately proffered by my brother Gordon that, under excessive stress, the glass door which protected the film within this compact projector might fling open, the man in charge went ahead. Turning the handle feverishly for fear he might be called to book for over-running the allotted schedule, we could do nothing now but stand by helplessly and breathlessly observe our pathetic companion with alarm as the projector rocked under such maltreatment.

I shall never forget the sound of breaking glass and the sickening smell of stripped fibre gears as the catch on the projector casing snapped, letting the glass inspection door fling open to meet the full impact of the handle.

This then, was yet another regrettable episode unhappily brought about by a tired old man who feared for his livelihood should he fall into disfavour with his boss by such an insignificant matter as running his show over-schedule. Having dedicated his life to the cinema was no guarantee that should the management 'turn sour' on him, he wouldn't be thrown out of employment regardless of his fast approaching retirement age, with no prospects of a living whatsoever. A sad reflection indeed, for what so many still call 'the good old days'. It was as simple as that, and how long this not over-talented person had 'eaten humble pie' to retain his position over the years, must certainly be open to conjecture. In retrospect, I now feel sure that had it not been for the good graces of our well-disposed employer at the time, this indifferent projectionist would never have 'stayed the course'.

It was shortly after the disconcerting incident with the projector that we also developed an untraceable fault in the main amplifier which eventually closed the show one night. Gordon and I assured the Chief we would gladly stay over and await the arrival of the Service Engineer who had been summoned earlier to rectify the elusive fault.

If the Chief looked tired when he left for home, undoubtedly, the sound engineer, when he arrived at the Roxy late that night, looked even more so. I remembered the man, of course, from earlier visits to our cinema and was struck by the fine physique of this Scotsman. This night, however, he was but a shadow of his former self, his weight-loss, for one thing, being readily apparent, while his eyes were red from lack of sleep through overwork at all hours.

The Scot was quick to express his gratitude that 'such wee laddies' should stay to assist him so late at night. We feigned indifference, I remember, telling the engineer it was as much in our interest to get the show going again, as indeed it was his.

Today, I suppose, you would call us 'good Company men' or something like that. Anyway, it was not until the early hours of the following day that the fault was rectified. It was during our late-night sojourn in the projection room, this matter-of-fact Scot related the strangest story I ever heard. Over a well-earned cup of coffee, he told us about his close associate and his hair-raising experience overnight in a deserted picture-house. How, as a direct result of that experience, his friend had suffered a mental set-back and was at that time under intensive care.

It all started, it seemed, when in a similar position as ourselves, there had been a complete breakdown in the sound equipment of a new super cinema in the North of England. The unfortunate fellow had been called to service the fault, only to find that no operator at that theatre was keen to stay overnight to assist in this direction. Firstly, the Chief made an excuse he simply had to get home on time as his wife was indisposed. The second projectionist, for his part, feigned sickness and just as quickly left the theatre, while any hope of the third operator staying was completely out of the question due to his age. The engineer was therefore quite alone as he prepared to investigate the fault, which other engineers could not – or *would* not proceed to this particular picture-house to try and resolve.

It was when the sound engineer was about to make a 'run' with his test film that the strangest thing happened. Without the slightest warning whatsoever, there was the unmistakable sound of Exit doors being flung open. He had rushed to the projection room windows to investigate – but all was still – the doors closed. The tough man he was, he hastened from the operating box to check the inexplicable phenomenon

44

more closely at the Exit doors themselves, only to find these correctly fastened with panic-bars in place.

Logically thinking and in order to outwit some possible prank that might have been foolishly played on him at such a late hour, the Serviceman satisfied himself by securely fastening the Exit doors with rope from the doorman's quarters. Having done this he returned to the projection room to re-check the equipment and make a further test run. He was determined, we were told, he had no intention of letting some irresponsible louts put him off his work, though inwardly he failed to understand how the prank — if this was the case — was executed.

It was on the second test run, however, the inexplicable happened again. This time, in a mood of both anger and bewilderment, the sound technician raced to the Exit doors, only to find them still safely secured — but the ropes broken! Being a man of stout heart as well as logic, even then he was convinced there was some cleverly contrived prank behind it all, and was determined to resolve the mystery — later.

Fortunately all was quiet from then on and having completed his duties in the projection room he decided to bunk-down in the comparative comfort of the theatre lounge until the early hours, when he would resume his investigation into the silly prank before returning to his lodgings where he had inadvertently left his door key.

Having slept but a few moments, he was startled into consciousness by terrified screams around him. Rubbing his tired eyes in sheer disbelief, he witnessed a mass of scurrying forms in wild confusion. Moreover, on closer scrutiny, the engineer noticed in horror, that the pathetic shapes that ran frantically before him, were indeed frightened people — and completely legless!

A moment later, now quite demoralised, the intense repugnance of it all eventually hitting his stomach causing him to vomit, he too, we were told, like the apparitions which screamed around him, took to his heels and ran from the eerie cinema into the welcome freshness of the night air.

"A clever prank by any standards," I had quipped bravely.

"I would like to think so," the engineer had put back with no trace of a smile. "But please let me continue, Geoffrey, there is more to it yet."

Indeed there was. For if the revelations by our Scottish friend had already proved startling, the follow-up to his fantastic narrative was perhaps, equally astonishing. He went on to explain how his colleague, still fired with indignation, if not humiliation at what he had experienced in the early hours of that morning at the cinema, had decided to return to the theatre for further investigation before leaving for his Head Office to hand in his report.

Back at the cinema, my brother and I were informed, the indignant man immediately confronted the manager, demanding an explanation for the weird happenings at the theatre.

The manager, it appeared, had returned an odd smile and after an apology for not putting his somewhat irate companion in the picture, went on to explain, had he realised the significance of the date, he would have naturally prepared him as to what he might expect that dreadful night at the picture-house. Furthermore, having agreed, with an air of indifference, that 'strange things' did occur once a year at his theatre, the manager proffered his own explanation for the macabre spectacle. Our companion then told us how the manager had withdrawn from a safe, a folder containing paper-cuttings and a couple of building plans.

"You will note from the paper-cuttings I have here," the theatre manager had pointed out, "that last night was the anniversary of a disastrous fire which gutted an old silent picture-theatre on this site." He had then taken both plans, placing them side by side. At once the full implication of this action was both readily apparent and startling. For here was a plan of the original theatre, clearly revealing one floor level for the lounge, while on the later plan of the existing cinema, the print called for a higher position for this accommodation.

"So there you have it," we were told the theatre manager had remarked glibly. "For what it is worth, my considered opinion after extensive research is that the terrible thing we have witnessed at my theatre, is — and I'm loathe to say this — the manifestation of the unfortunate people who were, God help them, involved in that appalling fire."

46

"Then," the sound engineer had countered quickly, "accepting your theory, the — the apparitions were, I suppose, following the *original* floor level of the lounge, hence the reason why I saw the horrific figures as legless — the lower part of these terrified creatures would be below floor level — right?"

The manager of this uncanny cinema had it seemed, agreed this was possible and indeed suggested his theory was the only explanation he, or anyone else for that matter, could put forward in order to resolve this supernatural phenomenon.

SECTION THREE

THE FIRE

It was soon after my brother, Gordon, and I had been
astounded by the tale of the devastating fire at the North of
England theatre, with all its uncanny side-effects, I was
approached by my boss and requested to take over the
projection room of a friendly opposition cinema, due to
their Chief projectionist being sick.

Now, if the idea that an exhibitor should go to such
length to assist an opposition house in times of dire need
should seem strange to anyone outside the business, perhaps
I ought to stress this was (and still is, as far as I am aware) yet
another example of the fine ethics of show people. Moreover,
in no way did my temporary absence from the Roxy jeopardise
the smooth running of that theatre, though obviously incur-
ring extra burden on my brother, Gordon.

Arriving at the Pavilion cinema, I was immediately staggered
at the neglect of the projection equipment and general
condition of the projection box, the access to which was by
a vertical iron ladder of the type I had heard about in my
earlier association with picture theatres. Even more to my
consternation, was the condition of the projectors themselves.
Not only was the film gate and sprocket deterioration on
both projectors so bad that film damage was almost inevitable,
but the projectors, though extremely robust and efficient if
adequately maintained, were nevertheless, somewhat of a fire
risk. For by the very nature of the design of these machines,
should the operator be unfortunate enough to have a film
break immediately below the top spool-box, the film would
invariably be fed directly into the arc illuminant, before the
projector could be closed down. A disturbing thought indeed,

48

Empire Cinema, Leicester Square

Granada Cinema, Clapham Junction

(c) *John D. Sharp*

Odeon/Regal Cinema, Edmonton

Odeon Cinema, Leicester Square

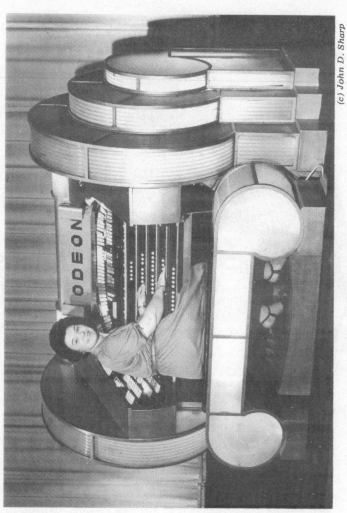

Doreen Chadwick at the console of the Compton Organ,
Odeon, Leicester Square.

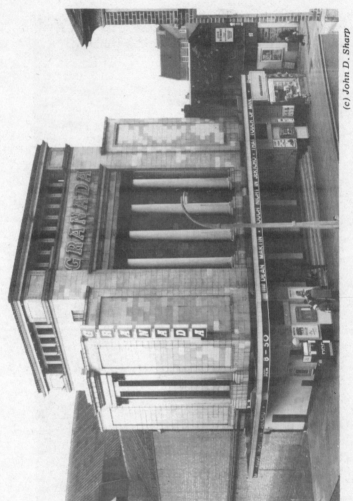

Granada Cinema, Tooting

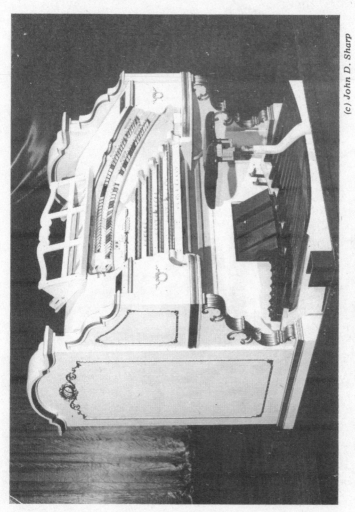

The organ at the Granada, Tooting.

(c) John D. Sharp

Gaumont State Cinema, Kilburn

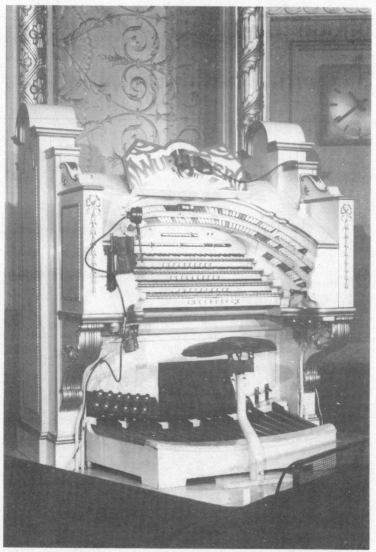

The Wurlitzer organ at Gaumont State, Kilburn.

(c) Hampshire Chronicle Group Newspapers

Theatre Royal, Winchester

(c) D.G. Carder

Example of conventional cinema sound/projector equipment.
Theatre Royal, Winchester

Modern conventional projectors at the Classic Cinema, Hinckley.

Example of modern 'Tower' apparatus.
Classic Cinema, Hinckley

(c) D.G. Carder

Example of a typical Rewind Room (conventional).

(c) John D. Sharp

Projection Room at the Regal, Ukbridge.

Example of modern 'Cakestand' equipment.   Regal, Sidcup

A Gretton Ward control panel.
Regal, Sidcup

Example of modern projector with 'Cakestand' equipment.
Regal, Sidcup

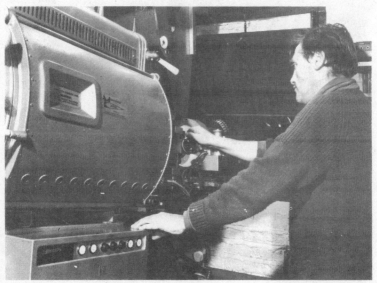

A man in the box at the Regal Sidcup.

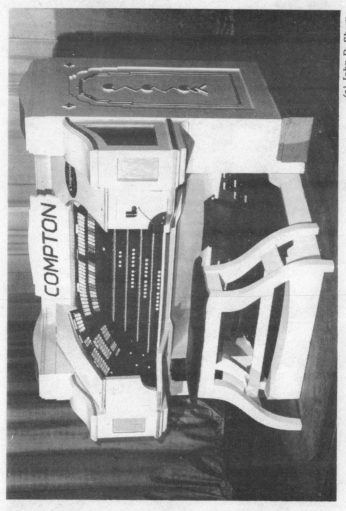

Compton organ at the Odeon, Birmingham.

(c) *John D. Sharp*

Odeon, Birmingham

(c) John D. Sharp

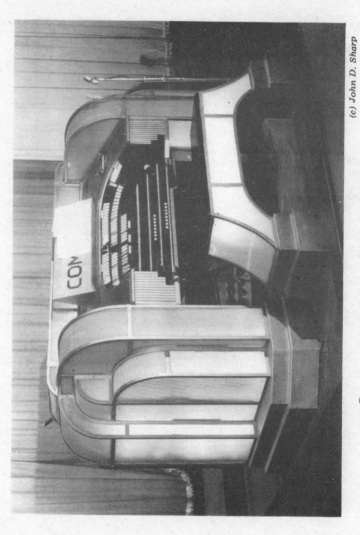

Compton organ at the Granada, Grantham.

Granada, Grantham

Projection Room equipment at Finsbury Park Astoria.

(c) John D. Sharp

especially with such inferior machines.

The first thing I did, therefore, was to ensure the fire-blanket (an asbestos sheet) was placed in close proximity to the projectors and that the fire extinguisher was serviceable, while not forgetting the inevitable bucket of sand. I observed too, the tell-tale scars of burnt metal in other areas of the projectors, indicating minor fires, which did nothing to put me at ease.

As if all this was not enough, on checking my programme I knew I was in for a rough run; for the feature film, though a very good box-office attraction, was nevertheless an 'oldie' which meant, of course, the film stock itself would undoubtedly leave much to be desired. It did. How much time I spent in my endeavour to make the celluloid reasonably safe for projection was anyone's guess. Even so, it wasn't without considerable trepidation I opened up on that picture later that unforgettable night.

I remember my willing assistant had left the projection room to hand-operate the tabs (curtains) at the interval, and to remain at his post until the certificate of the British Board of Film Censors flashed on the tabs as a cue to re-open the curtains on the feature film.

For my part, I had just left the 'dimmers' (a crude sliding-rheostat device for control of house lighting) when the unmistakable sound of a film break came through to me as the title music of the picture blurted raucously through the monitor speaker. I swung round quickly to see what I had feared might happen, had! The film, having snapped within the so-called safety enclosure attached to the top spool-box, was at that very moment being fed directly into the arc-housing. In the few moments it took me to reach the ill-fated projector, the entire projection room was enveloped in smoke as flames leaped ominously at the top box containing almost 2,000 feet of film. Instantly, I closed down the projector, simultaneously dropping the iron-clad safety shutters to protect the auditorium. The safety blanket, I recall, operated to some degree of efficiency as I released it from the canister. The extinguisher, regrettably, was of little use I found, this appliance being of a very inferior type. Remembering what Tony Barrington had

49

d

instilled in me, 'to keep the audience calm at all cost', I staggered across to the non-sync and placed the selected nondescript 'fire' record into operation which unobtrusively advised the management to be prepared to clear the theatre.

The last thing I remember about the disturbing incident was the arrival of the Fire Services, and the manager calling to me from below to come down at once, there was nothing further I could do in the box. Indeed he was right, for although I had managed to contain the fire within the projection room, the box at that moment was, without doubt, no place for anyone desiring the natural ability to breathe.

Miraculously enough, after the smoke in the box had dissipated and the fire Chief had given us the 'all clear', I found that apart from the burnt-out projector, the rest of the damaged equipment operated reasonably well, allowing me to finish the performance on one projector.

I think the greatest satisfaction I derived from this near-disaster, was the following night, when a patron remarked with an air of indifference, "I understand, Geoff, you had a bit of technical trouble in the projection room last night?"

"Something like that," I had responded nonchalantly. "I trust none-the-less, sir, you remained to see the finish of the show."

The gentleman, it transpired, had done just that, and was gratified to have seen the rest of the feature – yes, even with the 'intervals' required to change reels on one projector. Certainly, I found this patron's appreciation most stimulating at a time when it was most welcome.

While it is true, I suppose, that it is an ill wind that blows no good; much the same thing could be said about the occasional fire. Certainly in this instance, I am happy to say, it proved correct. For it wasn't long after my return to the Roxy, I learnt that the projection room at the Pavilion had been completely re-equipped with the latest in talking picture apparatus, much to the satisfaction of the long-suffering projectionists.

Moreover, at that very moment, the dire need for safety film in cinemas was being pressed forward by exhibitors throughout the trade. Frankly, it must be said, however, this otherwise commendable attitude wasn't entirely promoted by the natural desire for further safety in picture theatres, but also to enable the exhibitor to relax stringent rules and regulations which they found both irksome and restrictive. For instance, to quote but one example; if the necessity arose whereby an operator had to vacate the box for any reason, leaving only one other projectionist in charge, it was understood, he or another man would remain 'within calling distance' in case of emergency. There were of course, many other rules and regulations tightly knitted to meet the requirements of safety in the picture theatres in those hazardous days of the highly inflammable nitrate film stock, but I feel this example alone, is sufficient enough. For it was obvious to exhibitors, that once non-flam film was introduced into the cinemas, there could well exist a situation whereby — without endangering the public — a significant margin for reduction in staff was a distinct possibility.

In a narrative of this nature, I find it difficult at times to maintain a chronological sequence of events. However, be that as it may, I intend to proceed with this desirable aim in view, trusting at the same time, any departure in this direction will be received with good grace by the reader.

Accepting this then; upon my return to the Roxy, the next event of significance which comes to mind, was the exceptional interest in a controversial film we were about to screen. The picture (the title of which will remain nameless) was a somewhat crude attempt at revealing to the public the dangers of free-love in our society. I hasten to add, none-the-less, all the propriety of this time was embodied in this otherwise outrageous picture of that era. The sting of this 'epic', however, was very much in its tail, this being in the form of diagrammatic drawings coupled with outspoken dialogue between specialists in the field of V.D.

This best-forgotten film was of necessity first exhibited to members of the Local Watch Committee for approval, this in itself resulting in a farcical situation. For while certain members (male and female) of this commendable committee, eventually passed this picture for exhibition at our cinema, it wasn't until several had insisted on repeat performances in order to arrive at a just decision. Strangely enough, the fact that certain worthy stalwarts of this 'Watchdog Committee' fainted during the inevitable pre-viewing of this film, did nothing to influence their decision on the side of banning this picture in town. This fact alone, struck me as both remarkable and incomprehensible. However, it was agreed (as some measure of justification, no doubt) that at all times during exhibition, the presence of qualified medical attendants would be required in order to meet any possible contingency such as experienced by the Local Watch Committee themselves.

Eventually, this 'significant' production found its way to our projection room, and while our jubilant boss rubbed his hands together with satisfaction at the sight of the lengthy queues outside his cinema, we prepared our projectors for the 'film of the Century'.

Strategically placed within the cinema at the same time as we prepared our first screening of this lurid picture, were assembled a large representation of both first-aid and nursing personnel, the presence of whom would have more than satisfied the rulings of the Local Watch Committee. Let it suffice therefore, we were able, eventually, to open the doors to the eager crowd of patrons, the numbers of which far exceeded the management's wildest expectations for what was frankly a very poor film indeed. Truthfully, I am still convinced that had this wretched production been anything but a 'message' picture — without the tailpiece, it would have proved a complete loss at the box-office. As it was, this pathetic film had been extremely well promoted by cleverly slanted publicity which insidiously probed the innermost doubts of anyone who had experienced illicit sexual intercourse with a stranger. The truth of this statement, I believe, was adequately emphasised by the fact, that had the picture been screened *without* the harrowing tailpiece, it would have resulted in nothing more than a third-rate, second feature, in a double-feature programme.

None-the-less, as I have already indicated, the picture *was* a success — at least at the box-office. Moreover, it transpired, the medical attendants in the cinema were repeatedly called upon to render their services to patrons for whom the 'sequel' of the film proved too disturbing, to put it mildly. In fact, as I glanced through the projection room portholes during the interval between performances, I was surprised to note so many of our worthy picture-goers were in need of this attention, the sickness by no means being peculiar to the feminine gender.

It was later, however, at the close of the show, that I personally was inadvertently responsible for causing a near-riot. As was customary in those days, a suitable record was put aside for play-out use; usually a military recording which unconsciously expedited the departure of the patrons. It so happened, that having checked the record cabinet beneath the non-sync, our forgetful Chief operator replaced the carefully selected recording incorrectly. Subsequently, having 'played' the King on the tabs, I dutifully withdrew from the usual compartment in the cabinet the reserved record for play-out. Then having turned the volume control up to full blast with the intention of providing a hearty climax to an otherwise dreary show with the chosen military record, I turned to my other duties in the box. The next instant I froze. To my sheer consternation I realised I was playing a hit vocal recording of the day, the words of which stung at my ears with terrifying significance at what the top crooner of that time was unwittingly enquiring of our beloved patrons. For alas, the pregnant refrain of that unforgettable number, ran thus: *How's your Father and your Mother, your Sister and your Brother?*

As my brother Gordon, immediately aware of the *faux pas*, ran to the non-sync to change the unfortunate record, I was equally aware of the uproar within the auditorium. A moment later, our irate manager staggered sweatingly into the projection room, demanding in no uncertain terms, who was the bloody comedian in the box?

Happily for all of us, our good-natured boss decided not to wait for an explanation, and I for one, was much relieved to note a trace of a smile penetrating his flurried countenance as he turned about, to return to his honoured position in 'front of house'.

Whether our sordid 'epic' sex film did in fact get the intended message across, must be a matter of conjecture. I do know though, the plight of the young couple in a double seat of the back row of the circle, a short while later, is something my brother and I reflect upon with mixed feelings of both humour and embarrassment.

From our projection room portholes, we first became aware of an over-amorous blonde girl and her attractive male companion as they eagerly snuggled together in their seat even before the house lights were faded out. They were obviously desperate for sexual communication, there was no doubt about that. However, let me say right away, neither my brother, Gordon, or myself, were prone to doing a Peeping Tom act on our unsuspecting public. Indeed, in those enchanting days of cinema presentation – and I *do* mean presentation – there was precious little time to observe anything through the box windows, save the results of one's effort to provide the all-colourful embellishment required during an interval. Our dedicated sales girls too, expected and received the full benefit of our 'roving' spotlight as they perambulated the aisles with well-laden trays of confectionery.

However, there were nevertheless, the odd occasions, when having a few moments to spare, the projectionist was able to assess the 'volume' of an audience, thereby deriving satisfaction or otherwise from the brief perusal, subject of course to the 'state of the house'. This being such an occasion, my brother and I decided a closer peep at the passionate couple desirable. Although of course, the conduct of our patrons was no business of the projectionist, being naturally under the jurisdiction of the management, I decided none-the-less, an early appraisal of the situation by myself might be to the advantage of the young couple, and indeed save them embarrassment later. Moreover, the incredible configuration of these ardent lovers, had spurred my curiosity beyond bounds; it just had to be satisfied!

Accordingly therefore, I left the projection room and made my way into the hall and up the circle steps to the back row and turned my attention to my objective. Immediately I gulped in disbelief, for clearly outlined in the fluctuating ray of light from one of our projectors, I first noticed the

54

whiteness of the girl's legs spread-eagled across the double seat, while her blonde head hung limply over an arm-rest. Her companion, I then noticed, was somehow or other contorted into a crouched position above the prostrate figure beneath him. Furthermore, at this first moment of encounter, I couldn't decide whether the impassionate couple were trying to consolidate their position, or were attempting to withdraw from this singular contortion of vibrating togetherness. Perhaps even more incredulous in my opinion, was the apparent indifference of the patrons seated either side of the uninhibited couple. It was as though nothing untoward was happening between them that justified their attention — let alone, intervention.

While I was trying frantically to think of what I should do next, other than inform the manager of the 'disquieting' situation, I heard a whimper from the girl. "Please — please help us," she pleaded pathetically, "we are stuck." Not without considerable embarrassment I might add, I proceeded to weigh-up the position the best I could. Fortunately, this being the back row of the circle, I was able to consider the plight of the desperate young lovers more closely while maintaining a certain degree of obscurity from the rest of the nearby patrons. None-the-less, the hitherto disinterested picture-goers in close proximity to their undisciplined companions reacted immediately by turning their heads in my direction as I made a renewed appraisal of the disturbing incident.

It was at this juncture I realised the full predicament of the foolish couple. While endeavouring to make a closer physical 'contact' with each other in the restricted space of the cinema seat, their desire for sexual satisfaction was in no way supported by the inadequate strength of the seat frames which had collapsed under such maltreatment. It was at that moment, Clara, an usherette appeared and discreetly flashing her torch, cried, "Oh, my God! What's happened here, Geoffrey?"

The young girl, panting gaspingly under the weight of her perspiring lover, looked up at us sheepishly as Clara cradled the girl's blonde head in her hands, while I proceeded to help the young man to his feet.

"Shall I call the manager?" the attentive usherette had enquired a moment later. She had confronted the trembling, red-faced girl. "You might need medical attention."

I remember thinking (perhaps unkindly) if not now, maybe a few months later, but remained silent, of course, satisfied at least that 'capable Clara' had taken over control of the unseemly episode of the couple in the double seat.

As I returned to the projection room, I sensed a feeling of disgust for the man who had subjected his fair companion to such absolute humiliation and disgrace in a public place of entertainment, without a single word in defence of that very girl he physically claimed to love.

I didn't know it then, of course, but even this lamentable incident in the cinema was to be proved relatively insignificant by comparison to what I was to encounter later.

It was about this time, my brother, Gordon, and I became aware that our congenial boss had belatedly become concerned regarding his ever-increasing weight problem. I think perhaps the day this exhibitor decided to purchase a new motor car must have induced him to take a crash-action slimming course, rather than the rigorous advice proffered by his doctor. Indeed, the fact that his trusted medical practitioner (we were given to understand) had repeatedly stressed that without appropriate action to reduce the excess weight, the result might well prove fatal under certain conditions, in itself had little effect upon the stubborn nature of this showman. That was of course, until he found he was unable to place himself comfortably behind the steering wheel of the car of his choice, due to his corpulent waistline.

My personal appreciation of this gentleman's last-ditch stand to throw off his extreme fat, was on the occasion I visited the Hippodrome one morning for a chat with one of my colleagues. While 'talking shop' with my friend I suddenly became startled by a disturbing rumbling sound in the close proximity of the projection room. With some alarm in my voice, I remember, I asked my companion who at that moment was nonchalantly cleaning a projector, to account for the inexplicable 'earth tremor'. For an answer he jerked his head upwards to the area of the flat above I knew so well, at the same time suggesting I took a peep for myself. So doing, I ventured to the stairway leading in the direction of the nostalgic apartment. Immediately I halted in my tracks as I gazed with utter disbelief at the scene which confronted me. For not unlike a young schoolgirl in the playground of a preparatory school, I encountered my worthy boss skipping frantically, while large beads of perspiration covered his calf-clad anatomy. Dressed only in white shorts and slippers, this heavy man bounced with incredible rapidity upon the narrow landing before his flat, while completely oblivious, it seemed, to the noisy vibrations for which he was responsible.

I learnt later, this energetic person had taken also to running up and down stairs in a further attempt to 'lessen the load'. Whether this action was medically prudent, to say nothing of his skipping routine, I never did know. I do know though, that this grand old showman never lost his enthusiasm for dashing between his picture theatres to keep his staff on their toes. I assume therefore, his overall effort to at least maintain his already extravagant weight within reasonable limits was to some degree successful. Moreover, much to the satisfaction of this gentleman (and in no small way a considerable fillip to his ego, I was given to understand) he was able eventually to accommodate his bulk behind the steering wheel of the car he desired. This vehicle too, I might add, had to be conspicuously finished in a checker-board design with bright yellow flashes, to meet the requirements of this flamboyant character.

By the way, while I am on the topic of transport, I feel it would be very remiss of me indeed to omit reference to the valuable service maintained throughout the Golden Era of Talking Pictures (and since!) by the F.T.S. (film transport service), the truly vital link between the film renters and the scattered cinemas throughout the entire country. As always, any association with the cinema, no matter how seemingly remote from the actual presentation of films, invariably claimed never-lacking interest. In retrospect therefore, I feel it was only natural that when the opportunity occurred for me to accompany a film transport driver on an excursion to the Wardour Street film vaults and subsequent delivery of films in his area, I was both ready and willing. At this point, I feel I cannot proceed without a word of admiration for the driver of that particular transport, who was as much dedicated to his job of providing prompt delivery of pictures to the cinemas as my brother Gordon and I were dedicated to exhibiting them. The fact too, that this remarkable middle-aged, under-sized Cockney − no more than five foot two − could manipulate the heavy and cumbersome film transit cases with such apparent ease, still remains a mystery to me. Furthermore, the sad episode in his life, for which this spritely character made no apology for relating during our many hours together in his noisy cab, did nothing to dampen his cheerful attitude to life. The fact that his bride-to-be had jilted him at the last moment for the security of a nine-to-five clerk with more compatible hours, seemingly did nothing to embitter him. Indeed, as we sped through the night, my companion constantly checking his battered watch to verify punctuality, he would chant in his cheerful but raucous voice, the ditty of the day, no other than the one which ran: *Somebody Stole My Gal.*

Coincidently enough it would seem, it was but quite recently, while engaged in the writing of this book, I was fortunate enough to hear (with no little nostalgia, I must confess) an old recording of that very number, which I have always associated with that remarkable, resilient Cockney character.

Anyone outside the cinema might find it difficult to believe that apart from the front of house staff and attendants, the projectionist too, with but an occasional peep into the auditorium, can, after a while, become aware of certain regular patrons and their peculiar behaviour: none-the-less, I assure you this is so. For instance, I recall a slim, sad-faced brunette, for whom a seat in the cinema was the time and place to throw off her shoes with the apparent cares of the day, and relax in an air of complete abandonment. For many, I feel sure (other than the obvious love makers who don't come to see the picture anyway), a seat in the cinema was, and still is I suppose, synonymous with the kind of dream world in which, but for the harsh realities of life, so many of us would like to participate. In other words, the picture theatre by the very nature of its development and existence, is unquestionably a haven of escape from the frustrating routine of our daily duties, where we may exist, if but for a few carefree hours, in the comfortable world of make-believe. At the risk of digressing for a moment, I would add; no other medium of entertainment (as far as I am concerned, anyway) can parallel the 'magic carpet' effect of the seat in the cinema. Immediately I hear someone talking over my shoulder: "What about television?" My equally quick rejoinder to this person is quite simple, yet I am sure, none-the-less an accepted fact. For as far as TV is concerned, we are surrounded, are we not, with the very material reminders in our home of our prosaic existence from which we are trying so desperately to escape. The fact remains therefore, that within the all too familiar precincts of our environment, we are not *conditioned* for our 'flight to fantasy' as we stare at the 'box' in the corner of the room. To underline the point I am striving to put over, let us reflect for a moment on a picture we first saw at our local picture-house, then later on TV. I have no hesitation in suggesting that our immediate reaction is invariably one of keen disappointment. Now I cannot accept for one moment that this very picture, first enjoyed at the cinema then later transmitted on television, has lost impact simply because of the time factor between exhibitions, nor for that matter, due solely to the smallness of the home screen. No, the production is *still* the same, the stars are *still* as good, and of course the screenplay could not have lost its story-line. In other words, it is still the same fine picture — but with an important exception; the loss of *atmosphere*, the vital 'magic carpet' to carry us away into the world of make-believe, in which we desire to be transported from time to time. Yes, I am sure, it is as simple as that.

For all this (as I have previously indicated) there are others who would use the cinema for a far different purpose altogether, be it merely to sneak away into suitably conditioned seclusion with illicit companions, while he or she should be at home with their respective spouse; or those for whom I would simply classify as 'mystery couples'.

Unlike the lovers in the circle, to whom I have already referred at some length, the odd couple who come to mind more readily than most, were the apparently very sedate middle-aged pair who invariably occupied the same double seat directly beneath my particular projection room porthole. With a courteous smile and bow to the picture-house staff as they entered the theatre during the illuminated sales interval, they would eventually accommodate themselves with the refined natural dignity of royalty, in their accustomed seat. The woman, for her part, would proffer a gentle flutter of her gloved hand, in unison with her regal smile to the receptive acquaintance placed some few rows before her. Her companion, a seemingly over-fed, red-faced male with a distinctive air of superiority about him, would do no more than stand at attention until his voluptuous companion had sententiously lowered herself into her seat. It could be said, quite rightly of course, the attitude of this dignified pair in public amounted to nothing more than the desire of such people to be recognised readily by those around them. Well, as far as that goes it certainly worked for me, be it merely through the window of the projection room, otherwise it follows, does it not, I would not be relating this episode at all. But to continue; to my surprise, it soon became a ritual of this odd couple to vacate their seats the moment the feature film hit the screen! At first, perhaps naturally enough, I took little notice of this somewhat unusual exodus at the peak of their entertainment, believing the couple had suddenly remembered something of paramount importance which could not possibly wait. Indeed, I recall the highly irresponsible newly-married pair who dashed hot-footed to the pictures to see their film idols, only to return home later to find their cherished residence flooded: they'd left the plug in the bath – and the taps turned on! I soon decided, however, this could hardly be the case as far as this couple were concerned, for as I have previously indicated, for them this strange departure had become a ritual!

To say I became intrigued with these two characters, I must admit, would be a gross understatement. None-the-less, for a time at least, I tried to think this thing out in a casual sort of way, refusing to put any elaborate emphasis on the continued strange behaviour of these people, while there might have existed for all that, a simple explanation for what appeared at the time, quite inexplicable. Logically, however, I later reasoned with myself, that no one but a fool would pay good money at the box-office to see but half the entertainment for which they paid. It just didn't make sense. Nor for that matter, could the conditions within the cinema, in any way justify the untimely departure. Moreover, although mid-summer at the time, it is true to say the theatre air-conditioning plant was functioning perfectly, providing, astonishingly enough, a more inviting atmosphere within the theatre than outside.

Alas, I eventually came to the somewhat unkind conclusion the odd couple must either be 'ninepence to the shilling' or had a very good reason for what they were doing: I favoured the latter. With this uppermost in my mind, I therefore made myself available (with the co-operation of my brother Gordon) to make my usual theatre check at the precise time of the next 'strange exodus'.

Discreetly following the sedate companions at a convenient distance when the time arrived, I was surprised to find that on leaving the auditorium, these truly strange characters did not in fact make to leave the cinema. Nor for that matter, was the lounge or confectionery kiosk their possible objective. No, to my sheer consternation, they calmly side-stepped into the doorway which led via stone steps – to the boiler room! At this juncture I paused at the top of the stone stairway, by no means sure of my next move, for irrespective of the odd behaviour of those I pursued, I suddenly sensed a feeling of guilt for what I had previously so light-heartedly set out to do. Yet, rightly I suppose, I told myself that my first duty was to my employer and certainly no less to the rest of the staff employed by him. Who knew at that moment, I reflected dramatically, what these people were about to do? Sabotage by agents of an opposition concern, perhaps? Indeed, such underhanded exploits by some unscrupulous exhibitors were by no means unknown at that time, when the rivalry of the independent showman was at its highest. Not unlike the snoopers within other industries today, the cinema too,

61

had their fair quota of spys in the struggle for supremacy in the Golden Era of the motion picture. Certainly I knew of more than one picture theatre which suffered serious set-backs, to put it mildly, in those early days of the cinema, following 'casing' of a 'house' by an agent of the opposition.

At length, therefore, my conscience suitably vindicated by these ominous reflections, I proceeded stealthily down the steps and into the boiler room. The next instant, I jerked myself to a halt as I gazed unbelievingly at the incredible scene before me. If the encounter with the 'lovers in the circle' had caused me to catch my breath; believe me, the confrontation of the elderly couple, completely devoid of their elegant attire and very much in a state of sexual communication behind the theatre boiler, all but choked me. I remember backing impulsively up the stone stairway from whence I had come, my eyes still focused on the pathetic animations of the fervid pair as they sighed and groaned, quite oblivious to my intrusion and indeed, it seemed, the obvious discomfort of the pile of coke upon which they lay.

To this day, I am still convinced that neither my brother Gordon, nor for that matter, any other member of the cinema staff, held much credence to my story. Moreover, who could blame them? For in the first place, who but a couple of complete fools would go to such extremes to draw attention to themselves only to commit such a lurid act of indecency within the highly unromantic atmosphere of a cinema boiler room? In a strange sort of way, I suppose, these queer characters must have derived an odd kind of satisfaction in pursuing their sensualistic activities in such an unorthodox manner. Today, I imagine, the antics of such people would cause little more than a lift of an eyebrow. At worst, I am sure, they would suffer no more indignity than to be classified as 'kinky'.

However, be that as it may, I do recall that following that eventful night, the door leading to the stoke-hole was significantly kept locked, with keys provided to authorised staff only. I also remember, from that moment onwards, we were never again patronised by the presence of that odd, pathetic pair in our cinema. It could be assumed therefore, they had 'got the message'.

While such inexcusable incidents of complete lack of self-control were being perpetuated by some of our none-the-less valued patrons in some instances, on the other hand, the cinema staff themselves were now being subjected to even more rigorous rules and regulations than I have already indicated hitherto.

It would be true to say for example, by the very nature of the technical advancement within the projection room at that time, no projectionist other than a self-disciplined, dedicated individual, would have 'stayed the course' for long. But having dealt previously at some length in this direction, I feel it would therefore be very remiss of me indeed, not to put equally on record the highly commendable discipline and decorum of the front of the house staff with whom I am proud to have been associated.

Of course, there are many who still recall, perhaps with a touch of nostalgia, the man in uniform who once greeted us majestically on the cinema steps, but alas, like so many other refinements in the world of the cinema, has all but receded into oblivion. So far as the cinema is concerned, I am convinced this well-groomed picture theatre commissionaire has stood the test of time in more ways than one, and will be long remembered. Moreover, I might add, a similarly well-presented page boy, was by no means an exception to the rule in the heyday of talking pictures when it came to staffing a super cinema similar to the one in which my brother, Gordon, and I were employed at the time. But for all their smartness and apparent glamour, like the military man in uniform, behind it all there existed numerous arduous tasks and chores before they dutifully presented themselves at the appropriate time for the benefit of the public.

Now, having read about my association with a cinema usherette, one might well be forgiven for believing the following tribute and heart-felt respect for these cinema employees, as being unduly biased in their favour. Regardless of this however, it is my considered opinion that these remarkable girls, like the projectionist in the box, have been very much underrated in respect of their contribution to the successful development of cinematograph entertainment.

In the days of the cinema when 'presentation' and 'status'

was paramount in most cinemas, I have no hesitation in stating this all important hallmark of a first-class show, was by no means entirely in the hands of the projectionist. Indeed, without an efficient and dedicated staff outside the projection room to establish good relations with the public, the efforts of the man in the box were bound to lose much significance. So much so, in fact, it soon became quite clear to the proprietors of leading circuits throughout the country that above all else, the picture-goer must feel both welcome and suitably 'conditioned' in readiness to receive full satisfaction from the picture he or she had come to see. And few did more to establish this vital aim and the serene dignity of the picture theatre than the charming usherettes and sales girls, for whom, I repeat, like the cinema operator, their true value in the world of cinema has, to a great extent, regrettably been left out of the picture. I hasten to add, however, there were some to whom I shall refer later who indeed were soon recognised for their abundant charm and pleasant deportment, and perhaps, not surprisingly, eventually made it to the top.

In retrospect though, I think with the advent of the Super Cinema it was logical, I suppose, to accept the theory that the staff, with the fine ornate buildings of that era, should be equally sedate, if not as refined as the elegant picture theatres in which they were employed. Once again, it was just a matter of providing the correct atmosphere for the people who mattered most, namely, the picture-goer. At that time, the patron was considered as much more than just another person to occupy a vacant seat. Everyone was rated as equally important, from the dishevelled youngster at the midday matinee to the sophisticated couples at the evening performance. It therefore behoved the well-trained usherette to establish this worthy attitude at all times; and in this direction, I am happy to relate, she was seldom found lacking.

In those days, I recall it was once said by an enlightened exhibitor, (truthfully, I believe) that every picture-goer was a V.I.P. Frankly, it is my conviction also that much of the greatness of today's cinema can be attributed to this highly commendable attitude of cinema staff in bygone days.

However, I would like to elaborate particularly on the service and the 'behind the scenes' training of the cinema usherette and her integral part in the concept of the picture-house. Right from the days of the fairground bioscope, it would be both justified and logical to suggest, there had to be someone responsible for attending to the patrons requirements and comfort, meagre as well it might have been in the embryo days of motion pictures. None-the-less, by the very nature of public entertainment of this sort, the fact remains, someone somewhere has to be responsible for the goodwill and welfare of the public from whom the showman makes his livelihood. Hastily, however, I must concede the fact that in the hectic days of the 'one man show', the role of the usher was invariably a question of 'one of the family' standing-in (among many other allied activities as previously recorded in this book) as an accepted way of life. Indeed, I remember the occasion, not without some embarrassment, I might add, when I, myself, 'stood-in' for an usherette/sales girl when this member of our 'mini-staff' was indisposed. My part of usher, I remember, was in no way disconcerting in some early days at the cinema, for on many occasions I had been 'shanghaied' to take tickets at the door, preceding my normal duties in the projection room. However, when it came to perambulating the aisles in the intervals with a laden tray of confectionery to be greeted by wolf-whistles and cat-calls from the younger members of the audience, I found it extremely difficult to light-heartedly counter their outrageous reception with a fixed grin of indifference. My quip-like rejoinders I bravely provided with the requested refreshments by these otherwise good-natured teenagers, I am sure, helped me through this unenviable situation.

But later, however, with the phase-out of 'the one man show' and the introduction of picture palaces in the true sense of the word, a well-trained floor-staff became as much an important part of the modern cinema as the projectionist in the box. The heyday of the usherette had arrived — with a completely over-due, well-earned status. Now with the emphasis on glamour, the 'prestige' circuits were insisting on much more than the 'run-of-the-mill' girl to adorn their theatres flamboyant auditoriums and serve the then discerning patron. Each and every girl was carefully chosen, not only for her ability to endure long hours whilst deprived of her normal social life outside the cinema, but for her natural talent and charm in dealing with the public. To elaborate this point, I know of one cinema manager at least, who spent more of his time recruiting 'the right kind of girl for the job', than he did in engaging the entire staff for his projection room! Once engaged, 'the girl' was subjected to strict rules and regulations, the severity of which had to be witnessed to be believed. Surprisingly enough, though, despite the military-like obligations imposed upon these girls, seldom did a girl quit without her post being immediately filled by another young lady anxious to become a picture theatre attendant. Like the bright light of The Electric Picture Theatre which in my youth had been instrumental to some extent in inducing me into the projection room, much the same, I believe, was the case of these romantic young girls, drawn moth-like into the film 'factories' of make-believe.

I think the best way in which I can describe the kind of discipline these cinema girls gladly accepted in their role of 'Super' usherettes, is to quote from a notice I recall reading with consternation when repairing an electrical fault in one of their staff rooms. On looking back, it still surprises me, incidently, that so many cinema employees (and this most certainly includes myself, by the way) conceded to such dictatorial whims of certain bosses, just for the doubtful 'honour' of working in a picture theatre. I hasten to add, of course (as mentioned earlier in this work) the N.A.T.K.E. (National Association of Kinematograph and Theatrical Employees) did much to 'even the score' as it were, but nevertheless, the balance almost always came down very much in the proprietors favour. And as far as I can ascertain from my contacts still in the industry – still does! However, to get back to that notice in the perfume-saturated staff room of bygone days. As I remember the placard read something like this:

NOTICE TO USHERETTES/SALES STAFF

1)   Punctuality is essential in order to maintain the

smooth running of this cinema. This must be adhered to at all times.

2) Smartness and cleanliness is naturally of great importance. In this respect, sales girls, in particular, should pay meticulous attention to their finger-nails. While the use of cosmetics is permissible, this adornment should be used with discretion and in a manner not likely to offend the patron's comfort or pleasure in any degree.

3) Girls will parade for inspection by the Manager or his Assistant prior to each performance at the times requested by the Management.

4) Uniforms are the property of the theatre, and should be treated accordingly.
   Special attention is drawn to the following: Seams of stockings must — repeat must, be kept straight at all times. (Note: There is nothing more displeasing to the eye than a crooked stocking-line.) Matching hats to uniforms must always be worn without exception: this *is* part of your uniform. Hair must always be kept tidy also, and not allowed to fall into disarray when serving confectionery. Failure to do this could be both an embarrassment to patron and sales-girl alike, not to mention, highly unhygienic.

5) USE OF TORCHES: Usherettes should manipulate torches as indicated in adjoining diagram, namely; light from torches be directed DOWNWARDS, never UPWARDS thereby 'blinding' the patrons more than aiding them to their seats.

6) Sales staff will be spot-lighted momentarily during the intervals in order to enhance sales. It is important, therefore, you are at the *right* spot at the *right* time.

GENERAL REMARKS

Remember, a cheerful and friendly attitude towards the patrons is your paramount aim, for it need hardly be said, without the picture-goer, we fail to exist. However, any undue fraternisation by an usherette to a member of the audience, could mean instant dismissal.

Sadly, I reflect upon the incident when one of these 'Super' girls was severely reprimanded on parade by a supercilious ex-army officer, who obviously found a sadistic delight in humiliating the young girl in company with the rest of the staff. I remember the girl well; a perky little Cockney brunette with more high spirits than good sense, I am afraid. Eventually, I figured this unfortunate girl was sure to fall the victim of this unpleasant character who apparently knew next to nothing about dealing with the women under his jurisdiction. As young as this girl was, it was clear to me she found this shallow ex-serviceman as much of a bore as others did in the establishment. But regrettably in her case, she was too inexperienced to treat this wretched upstart with the contempt he deserved, and leave it at that. For instance, there was the occasion when prior to opening one night, she swaggered across the lounge mimicking this unpopular person with astonishing accuracy, at the same time giving army-like staccato instructions to the rest of the girls assembled awaiting inspection. Unfortunately, the Manager, appearing in time to witness the end of her performance was not amused. Instead of turning a blind eye to the incident or even a quip-like rebuke, he immediately vent his indignation upon the young usherette with a viciousness quite unwarranted to meet the situation. With sardonic rudeness and quite deplorable language, he soon brought the girl to tears. It was only the timely intervention of the Circuit Supervisor, who happily was visiting the cinema at the time, which brought the wretched episode to a satisfactory conclusion — in favour of the Cockney girl.

Incidently, the Circuit Supervisor who dealt so efficiently with the usherette incident I have just mentioned, was, herself, understandably enough, at one time a cinema usherette. This charming woman had been noted by a cinema executive for her natural aptitude for dealing with people a short time prior to her well-earned appointment. While not pretty in the true sense of the word, this person, nevertheless, had sufficient personality and decorum to qualify for the position she held so adequately. It should be pointed out also, that other usherettes with similar qualities and attributions for promotion, seldom failed to make the grade whenever the opportunity presented itself. Indeed, there were some who even climbed to the dizzy heights of stardom (not only in this country, by the way) in the medium of films themselves, but as might be expected, this of course was more the exception rather than the rule. Notwithstanding this, however, there were others I recall, who made the grade outside the glamorous cinematic world altogether, and perhaps gained even more status and satisfaction in the role of devoted wife with their spouse, first encountered within the precincts of the local cinema.

Now, if one should ask me why these particular girls, by the mere fact of working in a picture-house, should have accomplished so much, far removed from the seemingly insignificant job of usherette, the short answer is: I don't know. One might argue of course, the meticulous training of these 'Super' girls, coupled with their ability to withstand long, indifferent hours of employment, 'self-imprisoned' within a cinema, not to mention the 'charm-school brigade' of managements, with the fervent doctrine of 'be cheerful at all times', could well have had some significance in this matter. Others, of course, may have different ideas in this direction.

In conclusion to this sequence concerning the part played by the usherette in the highly successful days of motion pictures, I venture to suggest it was from this far-seeing new approach to the girl attendant, the idea occurred to a leading name in the industry that a similar scheme for the training of film stars was also a feasible proposition. It was not surprising therefore, the inauguration of special schools for the training of potential stars was soon to follow. Certainly, the 'Charm School' came as no surprise to me, being as it were, a natural sequel to the course of events I have already outlined. Undoubtedly however, there must be many in the cinema industry today, who might not concede this qualification for reasons better known to themselves than to me. On the other hand, none-the-less, there are I am sure, many who would be completely in accord with my analysis in this respect. Be that as it may, and no matter how my cinematic colleagues might care to juggle the 'chicken and the egg' to qualify their particular belief in which came first, one fact, at least, is indisputable; cinema today owes much to the courage and inspiration of those talented few, who through their ceaseless efforts are responsible for lifting the cinema out of the 'Flea Pit' category into the delightful palaces of perfection. It should be appreciated, incidently, I have but briefly covered the role of usherette in the picture-house, inasmuch as I have deliberately tried to play down her participation (believe it or not) because of my intimate association with one of them. For obvious reasons, as I believe I have previously suggested, when one is so closely involved in a situation of this nature, it is difficult to be completely unbiased. I therefore consider it prudent to close this reference at this juncture, rather than over-play my hand in this respect. This accepted then, I shall disregard the temptation to elaborate further on this subject, justifiably or otherwise, and turn now to a macabre experience which nevertheless I feel should be included in this book.

It was in the height of Summer, when not only is the projectionist flagging under the heat from the arc lamps in the close proximity of projection rooms, but 'sweating it out' outside also, the public were anxious to take full advantage of our much-publicised cool, fresh-air plant within the added comfort of the theatre auditorium. It was no misrepresentation either; the atmospheric conditions inside the hall were indeed ideal compared with the sweltering heat outside the building. So, ironically enough, with an indifferent picture on our screen and Natures climatic opposition to

70

indoor entertainment of any kind prevailing outside, unbelievably, we were playing to packed houses. On the night in question we had developed an electrical fault in the motor which operated the tabs (curtains). Of necessity therefore, in the manner of earlier days, the tabs had to be manually operated until my brother Gordon and I could find a suitable opportunity to rectify the breakdown. With no little sense of annoyance on this occasion, I must admit, for having to leave the box and proceed to the other end of the theatre after experiencing a particularly fatiguing day, I accordingly made my way in good time to take my position backstage in order to draw the tabs on cue, as the King 'hit' the screen. By the dim light of a shielded blue lamp I switched on when I arrived at my post to enable me to disengage the unserviceable tab motor, I took my stance in readiness for my cue. Then dutifully glancing around to check if everything was in order, I immediately froze. In the eerie glow of the obscure inspection lamp, I saw the ominously still form of a big man, his disturbing eyes wide open and keenly penetrating. He lay outstretched on the floor, his tousle-haired head supported only by a makeshift pillow of a tattered jacket, presumably his own, as the figure was jacketless. I remember, most vividly and with a twinge of embarrassment, how unceremoniously I hastily closed the tabs at the end of that performance, before I hurried in search of the assistant manager who was in charge of the cinema at that time.

No less do I recall the humiliation of ridicule before other members of the staff which I received from this self-opinionated humbug as he explained the situation. "Why, you silly chap," he had flung back at me after my breathless explanation of what I had encountered backstage but a few moments previously, "For your information," he had taunted condescendingly, "the stupid chap was intoxicated. In order to prevent the damn fool spoiling the entertainment for the rest of the audience, I had him taken behind the screen, where undoubtedly he is still trying to sleep off his drunken stupor. Satisfied?"

Indignantly, with the bravado of youth, I told the man I was very far from satisfied and in his own interest, he had better take another look at the wretched person, drunk or otherwise.

With a meaningful sigh of resignation, the assistant manager said something like: "Oh, very well then, my lad. I suppose it is time anyway that I roused the fellow and saw him off the premises." I ignored the irritation of his overbearingness with effort as I followed the penguin-like character with a contemptuous smirk on his face, backstage. Once behind the tabs, the assistant manager bellowed with what he undoubtedly considered his most authoritative voice: "Come on now, my man, it's time you roused yourself and got going." On receiving no reaction from the prostrate figure behind the ornate proscenium, my companion and I hastened our steps to investigate further, though even at that juncture, as indeed I had already indicated, I feared the worst.

At length, the assistant manager straightened himself after bending low over the still figure, and in a voice which was far removed from the confident tone he had used but a few moments earlier, gasped; "My God, Geoffrey, you're right, the man *is* dead."

After that, as far as I can recall, everything seemed to happen at once. Both ambulance and police arrived simultaneously and many pointed questions were asked the moment the unfortunate person had been whisked away.

Above all else relating to this sombre event in the cinema, I shall never forget the impact it made upon the undermanager. The 'incident', in fact, shattered his confidence completely. Certainly (and I think quite justifiably) the wisdom of putting a man considered to be intoxicated and therefore not responsible for his actions, behind the tabs unattended, was very much open to criticism. For both the welfare of the man himself and more importantly, the safety of the entire audience had been put in jeopardy. Once again, had it not been for the tolerance and understanding of the great man himself, for whom I also worked at the time, I have no hesitation in believing the assistant manager would have been directed to the nearest exit, and that would have been that. As it was, following a suitable reprimand, he was permitted to continue his employment with the company, and to my surprise, having nonchalantly accepted the censure from the boss, he proved to be a far

(c) John D. Sharp

Reginald Dixon at the organ.
Abbey Hall, Abingdon

Reginald Dixon at the Wurlitzer colsole.

H. Robinson Cleaver at an organ console.

(c) *John D. Sharp*

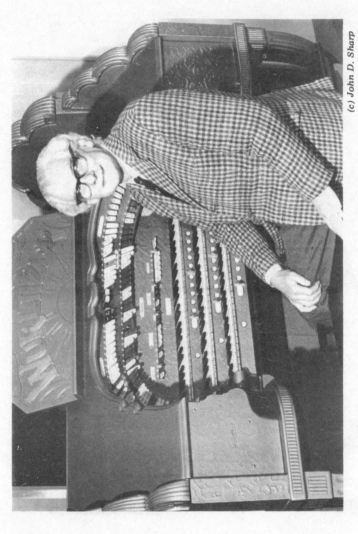

Robin Richmond Diss (Kitchen Bros) Garage, Norfolk.

Robin Richmond at the console of a Christie organ.

Leslie James at the organ console at the Rialto, Coventry.

(c) John D. Sharp

Organist Harold Smart

Organist Reginald Porter-Brown

View of organ pipework at the Trocadero Cinema,
Elephant & Castle.

View of organ pipework at the Ritz Cinema, Chatham.

(c) John D. Sharp

*Chamber view of organ pipework
at the Granada, Dartford.*

(c) John D. Sharp

*Further example of cinema organ pipework
at the Regent, Stutfold.*

Christie organ at the Regent, Poole.

Christie organ at Lonsdale, Carlisle.

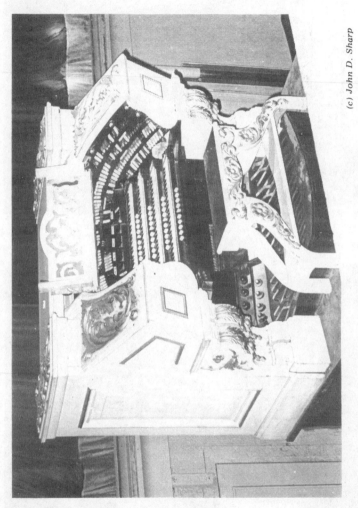

The organ at the Regal, Marble Arch.

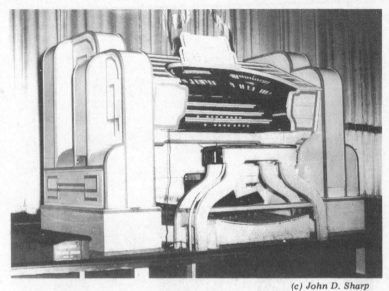

Conacher Theatre Organ at the Forum, Coventry.

Organ of Picture House, Paisley.

Compton organ at the Astoria, Folkestone.

Compton organ at the Odeon, Weston-Super-Mare.

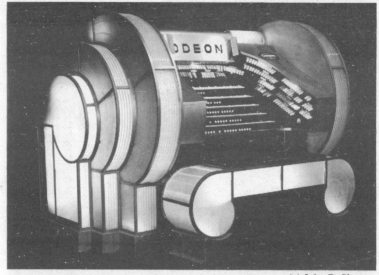

Compton organ at the Odeon, Leicester Square.

*Illuminated Wurlitzer cinema organ and piano
at the Ritz, Chatham.*

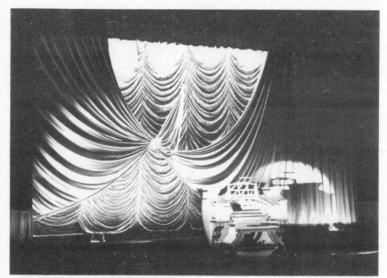

Example of tabs/curtains etc., Granada, Kingston.

Organ and organist at the Granada, Kingston.

Organ of the Regal, Newcastle-on-Tyne.

Organist at console at the Westover/ABC cinema, Bournemouth.

Gaumont/Odeon Cinema, Hammersmith.

Ritz Cinema, Ipswich.

*Further example of fine tabs/curtains and drapes etc.,
The Dome, Brighton*   (c) John D. Sharp

(c) John D. Sharp

Gaumont State Cinema, Kilburn.

better member of the cinema staff than hitherto.

I imagine it does few of us much harm to be roused from our inner smugness and self-esteem, occasionally. Indeed, in all honesty it must be said; I, myself, was by no means an exception to the rule in my early days in the cinema, though I might add, there are no apologies intended or should be taken in this respect. However, let it suffice that when we finally parted company it was, I assure you, on the most friendly terms.

f

THE ARRIVAL OF THE AUSTERE CINEMA

It was just before the calamity of World War II that, in my opinion, the cinema had reached its peak of perfection, if not in slight decline. The writing was on the wall, or more correctly, on the screen. The truth was that in the same way as the industry had previously sought for something to replace the 'silents' — and came up with the highly successful talking picture — at this juncture just before the war, history was repeating itself in a manner of speaking. Like a woman past her prime, the cinema was searching for the 'extra something' to make itself more attractive. Although it is true, not only did the cinema more than adequately survive the war years, but after an earlier set-back, when at the outset of hostilities the picture theatres were recommended to close; later, during the war, they were playing to packed houses. Nor was that all, for both American and British studios were very quick to exploit the regrettable war situation by hastily producing wartime, morale-boosting pictures; like Mrs Miniver, In Which We Serve, Target for Tonight, The Way Ahead, etc., etc., which proved to be not only good box-office, but a much needed fillip at a time when it was vital to our war efforts. And indeed, in all fairness, here again the projectionist played no small part in this direction, while sweating it out in the operating box during many an air raid. While on this reference, if I may be permitted to digress for a few moments, I reflect with a smile whenever I think of the occasion when on a short leave from the RAF, I visited a cinema proudly presenting a very intimate love story. I remember the scene well, as a beautiful girl (throwing wisdom to the wind with her underwear) seductively undressed in her boudoir to await

74

the arrival of her passionate lover. While outside the cinema the wailing sirens had given warning of an impending air raid on the city, inside the cinema the audience eagerly awaited the arrival of the passionate lover on the screen.

At length, as the hero of the film lingered for a moment outside the girl's bedroom, the projectionist chose that precise instant to flash upon the screen the notice which read 'ALL CLEAR' superimposed on the picture. Immediately following the signal the lover hastily entered the bedroom, as the audience rocked with laughter. A morale-booster indeed!

But to return to the period just before the declaration of war in September 1939. Generally speaking, I was somehow disconcerted by the story lines of the films themselves at that time. They were, in fact, becoming exceedingly hackneyed both in plot and inspiration, and therefore quite unable to maintain the high level of cinema entertainment as enjoyed hitherto. In qualification of the statement I have just made concerning certain less attractive pre-war pictures I could do worse than put forward the fact that greater emphasis than ever was being pressed home on the importance of the advancement of colour in films, in order to 'recapture' the public. Notwithstanding of course that coloured films were by no means a new innovation in picture making, for as far back as the early 'silents', there existed various types of coloured prints; though few, I am given to understand these were very successful. But by now great names in the production of colour films were doing their utmost to promote (still further) the pictures where colour was the main attraction, and therefore could 'carry' an indifferent or trite story line. More than ever, trailers (pre-advertising of pictures to come) invariably put more emphasis on the colour process used in the making of the picture than the story itself! Indeed, such publicity jargon as 'Filmed in glorious Technicolor' etc., is but one example of the kind of eye-catching exploitation which soon became commonplace on cinema screens. I hasten to add at this juncture; the omission of any reference to other colour processing used in the production of these pictures is by no means intended as a derogatory reflection on the high quality of the productions concerned.

This point accepted then, I trust I have adequately provided some idea of the situation which existed at the time and the impact it made upon me, which at least suggested the cinema had to 'look to its laurels' to stay in business indefinitely. Moreover, it was while serving in the Royal Air Force during the war that I became disturbed, on my brief visits to the mess or canteen, by the quite unbelievable popularity of what I considered an utterly stupid pastime called housey-housey. Perhaps subconsciously, even then, something told me that this wretched game was to prove an unparalleled opposition to my beloved cinema entertainment as I knew it.

Upon my release from the Service, it was-of no consolation to me to find my intuition and fears were only too well founded – the era of the bingo hall and all it represented in terms of the gambling public, had arrived. And frankly, human nature being what it is, few could resist the chance of 'easy' money under the guise of entertainment. Like a prolific writer once said, 'He could resist anything in life – except temptation.' I too, would subscribe to his profound feelings in this respect, for surely the undeniable success of the bingo halls alone in the post-war years, is sufficient in itself to qualify the wisdom and truth of the writer's words, satirical as they may be.

True, for a while at least, I returned to what was left of the cinema as I remembered it, but none-the-less, the wind of change was painfully apparent. Be it only in a manner in which the hitherto embellishments of the cinema itself were being unceremoniously dispensed with, permitting the development of the disquieting austere look to take predominance.

No longer was it felt necessary, or indeed desirable, for instance, to elaborate the proscenium with ornate designs or use multi-coloured illuminations to enhance the focal point of the cinema, where once the charm and elegance of beautiful tabs were used with no little significant enchantment. In fact the use of tabs in some cinemas was now discontinued altogether, though in all fairness it must be said this action was necessary in some instances to clear the way for wider screens where no suitable space was left to accommodate this once valued adornment of the old-time cinema.

Mock-up types of prosceniums, not unlike children's cardboard cutouts, seemed to be all that was required to off-set the 'naked' screen, which in the earlier days of the cinema was considered almost obscene by any showman at the time who was worthy of his title. At this stage of the game, I remember it was becoming ever increasingly apparent that the attempt to re-capture the public with the renewed exploitation of 'colour epics' was sadly failing to maintain expectations at the box-office and exhibitors began searching frantically for even bigger and better ways to re-establish themselves favourably with those upon whom their livelihood depended, namely, the 'disappearing' cinema-goer.

Logically enough, one might think, it didn't take the back-room boys long, under such pressure, to come up with their own fervent answers and suggestions of how to stop the cinematic rot. Soon, every conceivable gimcrack idea was hastily pushed forward in a desperate hope that possibly history might repeat itself in the same manner as did talkies when they replaced the 'silents' of the silver screen. Alas, this wasn't to be however, at least not to the same degree as the Golden Era of Talking Pictures. Almost pathetically (at least as far as I am concerned) we had thrust upon us demonstration exhibitions of what was proudly heralded as three dimensional pictures, where each and every patron was presented with an abominable pair of 3D spectacles to obtain the desirable affect of the 'wonders of 3D pictures'. This effort, as I saw it, was doomed to failure (as indeed were the 'smellies' experiment in America, for obvious reasons I would have thought) simply because it *was* nothing more than a hasty gimmick at its worst.

Later, and perhaps more leisurely, therefore the better, we were then introduced to even more extravagant ventures into picture presentation to be tossed hopefully around the cinematic arena. Perhaps with more confidence than was justified by the motion picture industry, the cinema-goers were once again expected to respond eagerly to still further developments in screen techniques to be known elaborately as Cinerama, Todd A.O. Cinemascope, 70 mm wide screen systems — and goodness knows what else!

77

While it is true, I believe, the wider screens and stereo sound improvements did much to boost the attraction of colour films, none-the-less, the story lines of these pictures were seldom the better for it — and alas, sometimes even worse!

So perhaps naturally enough, in a still further attempt to entice the public back into the picture theatres, it seemed quite acceptable and logical to try the 'shock treatment'. And in this direction it was not without some considerable success. For instance, such well known film makers as Hammer Productions hammered it home with what I can only describe as quite a unique talent for the presentation of horror in movies. While picture-goers chilled and thrilled with tense excitement as they clutched at their seats, cinema proprietors were sensing a warm glow of satisfaction at the more healthy box-office returns. However it might also be true to say that a specialist can only provide a special service to meet a special demand. I do feel therefore, successful as these horror movies have proved to be that, by the very nature of their concept, they meet the requirement of but a limited cross-section of the would-be cinema-goer.

For others the shock treatment deemed necessary was perhaps even more basic than provided by my beloved Hammer Films, i.e. the exploitation of sex in pictures. Perhaps I should put in here, while I believe a sex content in a film can well enhance the success of that production that on the other hand, like too much of anything, it can also create a sense of nausea. This is why I think the makers of so many pictures of this kind have come unstuck at the box-office. It seemed to me that as soon as a clever film producer introduced sex element incidents as *part of the story line* and therefore built up the required emotions throughout the picture, other less competent film makers (undoubtedly having viewed their adversaries productions with envy) decided to 'put jam on it'. I feel it wasn't surprising therefore, the result was simply that this ill-chosen action left the majority of regular picture goers quite unable to accept such an affront to their finer senses, or perhaps a little sad — it not sick!

Nevertheless, the success of many sex films cannot be

overlooked, if only qualified by their returns at the box-office. But for all this I still feel they rate as exceptions rather than the rule. Moreover, even these 'accepted' sex pictures must not be confused with the films which are generally known as 'blue movies'. For these wretched films, I must concede, can give claim to demand by cinema clubs requiring this type of entertainment.

However, it is refreshing to know that as recently as I write this narrative, a 'club' sex picture was being exhibited together with an old Judy Garland picture (The Wizard of Oz) in the same cinema; and I was told that the Judy Garland picture was taking more money at the cinema than the blue movie. This fact alone must surely underline the theme of my conviction in this book, namely that nothing, but nothing, will replace a well presented story. It is as simple as that and I make no apology for any repetition in this respect.

Yet astonishingly enough (with the exception of a handful of really first class pictures) exhibitors, believe it or not, were obliged to concede there were just not enough 'good' pictures to be had. Perhaps this is stating the obvious in view of the fact that so many 'oldies' were being re-booked, not only for the cinema, by the way, but for television transmission also! And while it cannot be denied the 'leading houses' were holding their own, so to speak, it is also true to say that many smaller shows were going over in part, if not fully, to meet the needs of bingo to stay in business. As a matter of fact, one of my old picture theatres soon became an unwilling victim of this circumstance, yet even this last pathetic attempt to keep the doors open was, I regret to say, but very short lived. Sadly, the last I saw of this fine old picture-house was just a heap of rubble on a derelict site. The entire building had been demolished in readiness to be taken over by a leading chain of super markets, yet to spread grotesquely across the country. But even more distressing perhaps, from a cinema lover's point of view, was my experience while on holiday recently. While motoring through an old eastern counties country town, I sensed a pang of nostalgia when, on rounding a bend, I encountered one of the first picture theatres I had the honour of opening in that picturesque locality. It had since been converted into a prosaic car sales showroom. Large cut-price sales posters now replaced the once sedate ornate still-frames which had proudly flanked either side of the neat foyer entrance. No less, the name of this once delightful picture-house, was now substituted by the somewhat obvious title which read simply: 'Car Depot'. A sad moment for me, indeed. Filled with an odd reaction of disquiet at the changing scene of 'progress', I quickly turned away and continued on my journey.

Ah well, I suppose if the demand is for more and more motor cars, it is logical we make and sell 'em, though I feel we have already overplayed our hand in this respect to some extent. However, by the same token, I suppose it is even more important one must eat in order to accomplish this motorised Utopia, desirable or otherwise. Therefore I would be the last to condemn or criticise the store proprietors for what they obviously consider a major contribution to the basic requirements of present-day discerning society. It is as simple as that, I imagine, yet I feel even this vital need should not be taken out of concept in the overall appraisal of the necessities of mankind. For while I believe it is true to say that man does not live by work alone, neither, I am convinced, does he 'live' by food alone. And though I would be one of the first to admit there are many other alternative ways and means, other than cinema, in which one might derive mental satisfaction and relaxation, the loss of the grand old picture palace of yesterday and its artistic contribution to society, cannot be discounted or dismissed flippantly without an inner sense of deep regret by many picture-goers of this era.

However, exhibitors (still in business) strived hopefully to obtain the right kind of picture to re-establish their previous status with the public but with more zeal than success I'm afraid. Consequently it came as no surprise to me, that while they were endeavouring to survive the 'big screen depression', (despite all they did by sheer gimmickery or otherwise to try and beat it) they once again looked 'inwards' rather than 'outwards', to cut the cost of keeping their picture theatres open.

For instance, while in the early days of the cinema it was considered unwise to load any projector with more than

2000 ft. of film, (this footage, in fact, being the maximum capacity of most projector spool-boxes at the time) now, in order to meet the requirements of reduced staff, etc., an entirely new approach in this direction was soon to be effected. However, even as I write this reference, I recall that many leading film companies (having made the single reels far in excess of 1000 ft.), stipulated no attempt to 'double-up' singles should be undertaken by any projectionist, as this action required continued splicing (i.e. cutting and rejoining film) with the result of potential film damage and mutilation. And quite frankly, to some extent I think the film companies attitude to the film-loading of projectors (at that time anyway) was reasonably justified. On the other hand of course, the fact remained, the smaller the reels, the more changeovers required. Hence the desirability, if not necessity, of more than one projectionist being present in the projection room at all times in order to manipulate the numerous changeovers required. This of course is regardless of the highly inflammable nature of the film stock at that point in cinema history to which I have already referred at some length. It should be pointed out none-the-less, as soon as such apparatus as the very successful Easi-Fit device, for instance, was introduced, it was possible for any reasonably competent operator to make a perfectly good 'solo' changeover. Be that as it may, now that the fire risk in the projection room had been considerably reduced with the introduction of non-flam film stock, (as mentioned earlier in this book) the cinema exhibitors were then in a far happier position. Certainly, managers could no longer be accused of taking unnecessary risks by reducing their projection staff when the trade introduced greater (though I doubt better) means of film-loading projectors in order to up-date the revised requirements in the projection room.

Nor was this all, with the extended 'mobility' of the projectionist, due to these changes (and more to come) it wasn't long before the cinema owner reached the full potential of these developments.

Subsequently, I suppose I accepted the somewhat novel idea of the creation of Studios 1, 2 and 3, as a natural sequence of events. These studios, in the main however, were usually converted picture theatres, restructured internally to provide three smaller theatres in one. Economically, I suppose, a very sound idea in the days of cinema 'famine', when any cost-saving could mean the difference of staying in or out of business. Moreover, with *three* entirely different programmes from which the picture-goer could choose at the same time under the same roof, the concept must surely be worthy of some merit. But regrettably, in my opinion anyway, with all this redevelopment of these converted cinemas came the 'Frankensteins' of the projection room. All too soon we witnessed (not without some trepidation, I think it's true to say) the introduction of such abominable cinematic creations to be known in the trade as the 'Cake Stand' and the 'Tower' system. The so-called virtue of these contraptions was to enable the projectionist to load a complete feature film, if not an entire programme, on one projector! In effect, one might say, whereas in the 'conventional' days of the cinema an operator loaded a projector with, say, a couple of thousand feet of film at a time, now it would be more correct to say the long-suffering projectionist *inserted* a projector into literally, many thousand footage of film at one go! In other words, one might say, it was now a case of more film than projector! In view of this change even a layman to the cinema, I feel sure, will appreciate the added burden of having to manipulate such massive spools of film, be it for use from the horizontal 'Cake Stand' equipment or the grotesque perpendicular 'Tower' apparatus. Indeed, the make-up and spooling-off of these giant reels of celluloid may well be compared (relatively speaking, that is) with the changing of a Mini road wheel, before being encumbered with the task of handling similar equipment corresponding to heavy goods vehicles.

No matter, the exhibitors would still argue with a wry grin, the doubtful advantages of such a step forward in cinema technology. Vividly, I recall at least one pompous ass of a showman who was not reluctant to point out that with the departure from the early hand-fed arc-lamp, to the automatic-feed refinement, the projectionist, now also enjoying the labour-saving luxury of the 'Tower' and 'Cake Stand' device, had but little to do!

While I would concede obvious advantages brought about by this change in the projection room, I am convinced that no one but a fool, having worked this end of the film industry long enough to inherit the title of showman, would be so silly as to utter such complete nonsense. For now with the debatable virtues of release from the close proximity of the projector at all times, the man in the box was once again expected to fulfil numerous other duties, if only in the capacity of 'floating operator' between studios One, Two and Three! In effect, therefore, there now existed not only a staff reduction in may cinemas of this type, but also a bonus for the owners in a situation where one projectionist does the duties of three!

All clever stuff of course, as far as the cinema proprietors were concerned, but few cinema operators I feel, echoed the same joyful reactions. Indeed, apart from the technical changes within the projection box, with a three-show complex under one roof, operating at the same time, there had to be a very harsh re-think in regard to shift working of staff. Fair enough, with an adequate complement of operators (though naturally kept to the minimum) it was conceivably possible of course, to run the rota systems of these trio-studies with a reasonable degree of continuity without undue hardship to the projectionist. But alas, should an operator fall sick (or believe it or not) 'throw his hand in', one might well imagine the consequences to a tightly scheduled show rota, operating, in many cases, from ten-thirty in the morning until and including an all-night 'club' show. This unhappy circumstance of course, would mean simply that one or another unfortunate operator would be obliged to 'double-up' in order to keep the show on the sheet (screen).

Like Tony Barrington had once said; for a single man without matrimonial commitments, an unexpected re-arrangement of working hours at short notice was perhaps a situation in which domestic consideration mattered little. However, to the married man in the box, obviously such an unexpected turn of hours might well create an undesirable state of domestic conflict. For example (and at the risk of being dubbed a sentimental old fool) I wonder how many picture-goers enjoying a hilarious musical comedy in the cinema in which I was once closely associated, would have reacted had they known that the man in the box projecting the film was all but in tears. Unlike Tony Barrington, for this man, believe it or not, had greater loyalty to the picture theatre than to his spouse. As the operator left the house that night for the cinema, his wife departed also — for ever. However, both, I still fervently believe were basically delightful companions. But alas, the incompatibility of purpose in life can be all too disastrous between two such temperamental people when eventually the 'die is cast' in a cauldron of emotional conflict. Furthermore, I would be the last person to pass judgement on either one of this couple for the action taken in this delicate situation, for both, I feel sure, could more than justify the decision taken.

Let it suffice, therefore, the indisputable hardships of projection staff experienced in the earlier days of the cinema, have in many such instances, returned once again with the coming of technical developments and the introduction of the urgently contrived trio projection rooms, brought into being to provide an economic answer in the concept of the three-in-one picture show complex.

But if the projectionists were once again under pressure, so indeed were the cinema proprietors themselves. More than ever, the independent showman was finding it difficult to stay in business. Moreover, in many instances, even the 'panic' changeover to bingo failed to prevent a theatre from going out of existence altogether. Although (as already indicated in this work) many major circuits were able to survive the cinematic depression, it is none-the-less true that many smaller concerns and independent houses, were obliged to sell out and pay off their staffs; the sites and/or buildings being taken over as super stores or car sales areas, etc. Indeed, as I took stock recently while engaged in this work, I was dismayed to say the least, to note how many fine old picture theatres, even in my present locality, had either been demolished altogether, or at best (excluding bingo halls) converted for other use since the end of World War II.

For instance, following a brief survey within an area of say, approximately twenty miles, I recorded three complete cinema demolitions, two used for furniture and food storage, two taken over by a leading dance-hall syndicate, another put in use as a billiards hall, one as a multi-alley bowling establishment, plus three other fine old buildings, grotesquely boarded up, and as far as I can ascertain at this time, the ultimate fate of which is still undecided. Not a pretty picture.

Reflecting sadly upon this depressing data, I found myself (naturally enough, I suppose) ruminating also on the fate of the cinema staffs themselves, who were once associated with these one-time picture theatres. Consequently, it wasn't long before I succumbed to a singular compulsion to satisfy my desire to co-ordinate the one-time staffs of these 'ghost theatres' with their respective way of life today. A further spur in this direction, I must confess, was the strange feeling of disquiet that still rankled within me at a chance dialogue I overheard at an exhibitors' association meeting many years ago. Over a glass of scotch, a predominate figure in the industry, glibly declared his contempt for those who provided his very bread and butter — if not the occasional glass of whisky! The impact of this character's contemptuous remarks, uttered flippantly with an indifferent flip of a hand, is perhaps something others at that assembly have long since forgotten, but obviously not I, otherwise I would not be recording the incident here and now. However, to return to the point, when a reference was brought up at the meeting concerning the inadequate wage structure in respect of projectionist grading during a debate on the financial status of the then prosperous cinema industry. Quite unexpectedly, Mr X remarked sardonically, "My dear fellows, while I appreciate your concern for the chap in the box, please let us not overlook the fact that it doesn't require a degree in mechanics or showmanship to 'push a bit of celluloid through a projector all night'." He had chuckled. "And furthermore," he added, obviously very pleased with the astonished attention he was receiving, "remember, gentlemen, the operator has also the added bonus of free entertainment every night of the week. And I will tell you this," he had pressed on earnestly, a wagging index finger extending from the side of his whisky glass, "the projectionist is very much a loner; an animal, if you like, lost in a dream jungle of make-believe. Without his picture theatre territory, he'd be finished — and he knows it."

Such was the arrogance and conceit of a leading cinema personality for whom hitherto I had once held in high esteem. 'Without the picture theatre he'd be finished': I shall never forget that utterance. Even today I rebel inwardly that such complete nonsense should have been spoken by one who should have known very much better.

In the circumstances therefore, this added incentive very much to the fore, I proceeded to find out whether there might have been, at least, some element of justification for the opinion of this extraordinary showman acquaintance of many years ago.

Nevertheless, I trust it will be generally accepted that with the best of intentions in life, regrettably, there are also many disappointments. Therefore, by the very nature of things, try though I might, I was unable to trace but a few of the original staffs of the closed-down theatres I have indicated. However, the result of my prolonged investigations which were successful in this respect, left me in no doubt whatsoever that to flippantly classify a person's intelligence merely by his or her particular occupation at any given time, can be most misleading, if not downright stupid.

However to continue; in all walks of life I think it is true to say, there is always someone, somewhere, who can be relied upon to harbour a wealth of information, whatever its nature, just waiting to be released if suitably approached. With this is mind, it didn't take me long to come to the natural conclusion I suppose, that the best chance of obtaining the required data, would be to approach the oldest of my cinematic associates. Immediately, I thought of the 'old man of the theatre', as he was affectionately known in my immediate circle of picture theatre friends. This grand old man, long since retired from active show business, and expressing a wish to maintain anonymous by the way, was only too willing to help me in my investigations. Not only was he able to provide me with the knowledge of the achievements (or otherwise) of many of whom I was trying to trace by more devious methods, but also saved me valuable time and expense by supplying the answers on the spot to my persistent, if not exacting and personal research. I soon learnt, for instance, that the one-time manager of the 'food store' picture-house was still employed in a managerial capacity, though now completely divorced from show business altogether. No less successful, however, he had become an industrial executive in an engineering concern of some considerable repute. The chief projectionist from this food store theatre, I was told, had decided to leave civvy street shortly after the cinema closure and joined the Royal Air Force. Within this entirely different environment, it wasn't long before he too, was successful in gaining a commission in flying duties. Unfortunately however, my informant was unable to enlighten me as to the ultimate fate of the rest of the staff of this 'ghost' picture theatre. None-the-less, I was more than gratified to know that at least I didn't have to write off this initial probe as a complete loss.

But as far as the dance-hall 'cinema' was concerned, the 'old man' came up with a bonanza of information. Not only was I readily advised that the entire floor staff were more or less accommodated within the ball-room syndicate in one capacity or another, but he also provided a complete rundown of the projectionist's progress. This, I confess proved even more enlightening than I had ever dared hope. For while, of course, I gladly accepted the information concerning the re-employment of the rest of the 'house', the main purpose of my investigations was primarily concerned with the projectionist himself. Therefore, having received the other knowledge with both patience and appreciation, I was relieved none-the-less, to learn eventually that the chief operator of this one-time cinema had been fortunate enough to find a place for himself in one of the few remaining film studios still making pictures for the big screen. Another projectionist had been equally successful in obtaining a technical position with a well-known TV studio in the South of England.

Perhaps, though, the biggest surprise of all, was to learn that the junior operator from this now defunct theatre's projection room, had virtually hit the jack-pot so to speak. With his undeniable vitality and his uncanny appreciation of the pop scene, he had soon become a teenage guitar-playing idol in his own right, and was not only supporting himself very comfortably indeed, thank you, but also his widowed mother.

While I would have been prepared to let the foregoing suffice as sufficient evidence that the cinema projectionist can very well survive outside the 'cinematic jungle', I feel none-the-less, that any omission of reference to the current activities of my brother, Gordon, or indeed, myself for that matter, might well be misunderstood. With this in mind, therefore, I shall briefly cover this margin of possible misunderstanding by referring the reader to my previous comments concerning the war-time activities of my brother projectionist. Moreover, the fact that he is still very much associated with the cinema, obviously excludes him from further reference in this matter.

Now, of course, it leaves myself to be accounted for. But frankly, I have no intention of embellishing my own position or activities in any way whatsoever, simply because the very object of this work is to highlight the role of the forgotten cinema projectionist, and not — I repeat not, in any way intended to inhance my own social status in any respect. Therefore, to vindicate myself from any misrepresentation by omission, I will simply add this: Following my war-time service with the Royal Air Force, I found my horizon had been broadened in more ways than one. No longer could I condone the exploitation of personal liberty or loss of potential prospects, under the guise of dedication. (Perhaps the ghost of Tony Barrington had been talking in my ear, who knows?). Nor indeed, could it have been otherwise, as familiar cinemas around me became overnight bingo halls, or fell into disuse, leaving only a skeleton of major circuits.

With all this, and a forest of TV aerials grotesquely disfiguring otherwise pleasant-looking homesteads, if the writing wasn't on the screen, it was most certainly on the wall! In short, therefore, I fortunately decided to leave the cinema before it was mysteriously taken over by some concern or other — and later demolished.

Now, of necessity, I have my 'bread and butter' interests

in free-lance writing, from which I can claim modest success in the field of fiction. But that is another story.

This said then, I would like to conclude this record of my life as a cinema projectionist, with carefully considered reasons, why I, personally, believe the cinema still has a future and will continue to play a paramount part in our world of entertainment, for a long time to come.

CONCLUSION

If one consults one's dictionary for the definition of the word entertainment, it reads something like this: Entertainment; act of entertaining, reception and provision for guests, hospitality, that which entertains, amusement and a performance or show intended to give pleasure. Naturally (according to one's particular choice of dictionary) there are somewhat different interpretations of this word. As far as I am concerned, however, any credits in this respect should be made to my ever-ready 'friend', Chamber's Twentieth Century edition, a worthy, yet reasonably priced dictionary for general reference.

The point of all this then, is (I hope) to emphasise the nature of cinematograph entertainment in the concept of my overall appraisal of this subject. Quite frankly, as far as I see it anyhow, it scores on all points of definition. a) Act of entertaining — well it certainly does that! b) Reception and provision for 'guests' Yes? c) Hospitality — ah, now that brings to me an issue I would take up with present-day managements and one which I have already raised earlier in these memoirs. Something which in bygone days of motion pictures in our cinemas was deemed as essential as the friendly commissionaire in uniform, or even the manager himself. That something one was always happily aware of, yet couldn't put one's finger on, as it were; that reassuring feeling of really being wanted; every possible courtesy and comfort, in fact, being genuinly and unobtrusively extended with a natural air of goodwill. And that, believe me, *is* showbusiness!

So having, I trust, qualified my reference as far as entertainment is concerned, I feel I must once again refer to atmosphere, the all-important quality of any good show, including of course, any live performance as far back as the strolling players of the legendary Shakespearian era. Yes, without a doubt, atmosphere must rate very high in the argument for the continuation and indeed protracted promotion of cinematograph entertainment. However, having also dealt at some length with this issue previously in this book while on the topic of TV comparison with the big screen, I feel any further emphasis in this direction unnecessary.

Let it suffice therefore, it is my heart-felt opinion, that in the changing years of the picture show to come, any attempt, to 'sausage machine' this medium of entertainment by presenting it in 'cold blood', so to speak, is eventually doomed to dismal failure. If further proof of this argument be necessary, might I for one moment digress to offer a classic example of the fine old horse roundabout, once enhanced in all its splendour by the majestic steam-organ. Today, alas, this rare musical instrument no longer exists to serve its awe-inspiring purpose with the show-ground merry-go-round. After the departure of this fine old organ and its replacement by a less attractive musical embellishment, as with the departure of the cinema organ, so also departed the once-enchanted public. Indeed, I think it is true to say the great names in cinema organs following the steam organs, none-the-less, owe much to the development of the fair-ground bioscope and the elaborate ornate organ, once towed on tour from site to site. Therefore, by no means let us delude ourselves (whether we care to admit it or otherwise) that we no longer possess the inborn sense of desire to view and appreciate that which is beautiful. Strip anything (or anybody, for that matter) of that which attracts or gives pleasure by its essential or natural adornment and, believe me, sooner or later one turns away to search elsewhere for inner artistic satisfaction. For example, take a visit to any old stately home, ancient castle, or the like, and one will soon accept the fact we are all searching for an assurance that we still possess the inherited desire to appreciate that which is pleasing to behold, whether it be ancient architecture or a well 'presented' garden of a royal palace. And ironically enough, perhaps one is willing, if not eager, to pay well to view that which was once accepted as commonplace. Certainly I would be the last to complain about this continuing return to artistic 'sanity', for by the very nature of this trend, my argument is indeed strengthened beyond the use of mere words.

Very well, then; if one agrees with my analogy in this respect, one will I assume, also concede that nothing further be contemplated whereby the cinema is finally reduced to nothing more than its earlier counterpart, the penny peep show. Moreover, wherever economically possible, a realistic return to the former *artistic* status of the cinema must surely be the ultimate target of all genuinely concerned with the survival of the picture-house. In other words, with so many leisure activities to compete with in these days of instant entertainment and money-grabbing pastimes, the picture theatre is left with but one option with which it can re-establish itself in the forefront of show business. It is simply this: It is my humble yet carefully considered opinion that the cinema is now left with no other course to follow, than to return to the policy which made it such a highly successful family name in the world of entertainment. It must, I believe, no longer remain just another place of entertainment, flowing with the amusement tide, as it were, but restore itself to its elegant status of a picture *palace*. With this in mind, I feel confident the cinema has happily maintained a considerable edge on other forms of entertainment, inasmuch as it still provides exceptional value for money. For example, in what other form of show business is so much effort and expense expended to bring the final presentation before the public? Indeed (at the risk of departing from my earlier intention of no reference to the film industry outside the cinema itself) it is as well to reflect for a moment on what one *really* gets at the box-office for the modest price of a ticket to the stalls or circle.

First of all, of course, one is well aware that every picture that is produced demands the expertise of a very reliable film producer — and the operative word *is* reliable. For among his many varied duties (and believe me there are many) this man (or woman) has to put together the right kind of package deal to cover the entire concept of the production. In the Golden Era of Movies, perhaps not too difficult a task, with almost any banker ready and willing to underwrite what was then considered a very good investment indeed. Moreover (as in the live theatre) a persuasive producer could well influence an 'angel' (one who financially backs a production) to put his money behind a good story or film script without much difficulty. However, today, with inflation (be it only temporary) a very real menace to all forms of investment, gilt-edged or otherwise, the film producer must indeed be a person of very great standing and influence in every respect, to accomplish this desirable end.

Nevertheless, as undoubtedly with other forms of business ventures, the film industry, perhaps more than most, know well how to face up to such irksome circumstances with both courage and good sense of judgement. For even now, regardless of certain shortcomings I have suggested in this work, encouragingly enough, there are some very fine productions reaching our screens at this time by new names in the art of film making as well as those long established. Furthermore, the confidence and sound judgement of these enterprising film makers in such uncertain times, has most certainly been reflected by the success of their pictures at the box-office.

However, having dealt if but briefly, with the role of film producer, we may accept then that this worthy person has also engaged the equally valuable human and material assets of suitable writers, studio and location sites (if required) and staffs, many technicians including, of course, the invaluable cameramen, etc., not to mention a star or two upon which to 'hang' the picture, with his and/or her carefully chosen supporting cast.

This is by no means the whole story, for there is the inevitable addition of numerous and equally vital indirect staff required in the unique process of making a motion picture.

Let it suffice, therefore, without even considering the obvious merits of those who finally appear on our cinema screens, the cinema-goer receives considerable return for the money paid at the picture theatre cash office. For unlike many other forms of entertainment, what one enjoys from the seat in the circle or stalls, is not just a mere animated, talking picture, even at its best, but in fact an exhibition or portrayal of singular skills and much hard work, originally conceived then developed by 'behind the scene' people of indisputable foresight and inspiration in the art of film making – and no little tenacity, I might add. So, ragardless of the monumental cost of producing motion pictures in this day and age, I feel I have made my point that one, indeed, does get good value for money at the pictures – and the projectionist (without whom the entire production would become a 'dead loss') is there to ensure one gets it, too!

In concluding this reference to the cinema, therefore, I trust I may be forgiven for once again highlighting the very theme and purpose of these memoirs, which is, of course, to establish at least some measure of credit where, in my opinion, it has been far too long overdue – to the projectionist, the man in the box.

SOME GENERAL TERMS AND PHRASES
USED IN THE CINEMA

HOUSE Used generally to mean the picture theatre itself and/or such terms as 'a good house' (signifying a well-attended performance).

FRONT OF THE HOUSE Area upon which the Manager (or other 'front of the house' staff receive the public.

MANAGER ON THE GREEN Manager in front of the house.

LION'S DEN Manager's office.

FOYER Reception lobby immediately inside the cinema.

THE BOX Projection room.

SHEET OR POSTAGE STAMP The screen.

THE APRON Forefront of stage before the screen or tabs.

TABS Curtains.

PROSCENIUM Front part of stage and surrounding structure.

CATWALK Narrow footboard upon which to walk (or crawl) for purpose of inspection or cleaning house lighting, etc., in theatre roof.

BUCKETS Term sometimes used to refer to seats.

NON-SYNC Non-synchronised sound.

S.O.D. Sound on disc. (Records used in early talking pictures.)

S.O.F. Sound on film.

FLICKS More commonly used in the early days of moving pictures, to denote the 'flickering' characteristics of film presentation.

STRIKING THE ARC Term used for short-circuiting positive and negative carbons together momentarily, when carbon-arc lamps are used for projection illuminant. (Note: Then to be maintained at constant 'gap' as they burn away in order to ensure light perfection.)

95

CHANGE-OVER Transferring from one projector to another without interrupting continuity of picture or sound.

STILL FRAMES Cabinets for display of photographs (stills) outside or inside cinema.

A BURSTER Exceptional takings at the box-office.

THE BIRDS ARE SINGING Pay-day.

THE GHOST WALKS Persistent and unaccountable breakdowns in performance (usually in projection room).

P.R.S. SHEETS Performing Rights Society return forms denoting number of public performances of any recorded music (records, etc.).

A DEAD DUCK A very indifferent picture, resulting in poor returns at the box-office.

THE 'RAINCOAT BRIGADE' A term sometimes used to describe patrons attending a pornographic 'club' film exhibition.

PUTTING THE SHOW TO BED Packing-up films for despatch after completion of run (showing).